Nothing But Trouble Could Come From Kissing Flynn.

A woman as sane as she was—and the whole world knew Molly Weston was practical and hopelessly straitlaced—simply had more brains than to hurl herself off a cliff without a parachute.

But Flynn tempted her. As no man ever had. It was those eyes. It was that simmering, electric thing that shimmered in the air between them. It was that daredevil zest for life that captivated her, made crazy ideas come to her mind—like the thought that she'd regret it forever if she never made love with him.

He read her decision in her eyes. That slow, wicked grin of his faded. His gaze shifted from her eyes to her mouth, the playfulness disappearing from his expression.

Her hand rose higher, until her fingers were bare, naked inches from touching him. Her heart was suddenly pounding, pounding.

Until she heard the bellowing wail of a baby.

Dear Reader,

Where do you read Silhouette Desire? Sitting in your favorite chair? How about standing in line at the market or swinging in the sunporch hammock? Or do you hold out the entire day, waiting for all your distractions to dissolve around you, only to open a Desire novel once you're in a relaxing bath or resting against your softest pillow...? Wherever you indulge in Silhouette Desire, we know you do so with anticipation, and that's why we bring you the absolute best in romance fiction.

This month, look forward to talented Jennifer Greene's *A Baby in His In-Box*, where a sexy tutor gives March's MAN OF THE MONTH private lessons on sudden fatherhood. And in the second adorable tale of Elizabeth Bevarly's BLAME IT ON BOB series, *Beauty and the Brain*, a lady discovers she's still starry-eyed over her secret high school crush. Next, Susan Crosby takes readers on The Great Wife Search in *Bride Candidate #9*.

And don't miss a single kiss delivered by these delectable men: a roguish rancher in Amy J. Fetzer's *The Unlikely Bodyguard;* the strong, silent corporate hunk in the latest book in the RIGHT BRIDE, WRONG GROOM series, *Switched at the Altar,* by Metsy Hingle; and Eileen Wilks's mouthwatering honorable Texas hero in *Just a Little Bit Pregnant.*

So, no matter *where* you read, I know *what* you'll be reading—all six of March's irresistible Silhouette Desire love stories!

Regards,

Melissa Senate

Melissa Senate
Senior Editor
Silhouette Desire

Please address questions and book requests to:
Silhouette Reader Service
U.S.: 3010 Walden Ave., P.O. Box 1325, Buffalo, NY 14269
Canadian: P.O. Box 609, Fort Erie, Ont. L2A 5X3

JENNIFER
GREENE

A
BABY
IN HIS
IN-BOX

SILHOUETTE *Desire*®

Published by Silhouette Books

America's Publisher of Contemporary Romance

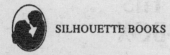

SILHOUETTE BOOKS

ISBN 0-373-76129-5

A BABY IN HIS IN-BOX

Copyright © 1998 by Jennifer Greene

Printed in U.S.A.

JENNIFER GREENE

lives near Lake Michigan with her husband and two children. Before writing full-time, she worked as a teacher and a personnel manager. Michigan State University honored her as an "outstanding woman graduate" for her work with women on campus.

Ms. Greene has written more than fifty category romances, for which she has won numerous awards, including two RITA awards from the Romance Writers of America in the Best Short Contemporary Books category, and a Career Achievement award from *Romantic Times* magazine.

One

"**W**hat the *hell* is this?"

Flynn McGannon had just hung up the phone when the whirlwind barreled into his office. "What's what?"

"You know exactly what." The whirlwind slapped a clipped set of papers on his desk. She pointed a royal finger at the offending documents, then at him. "There are words for men like you—starting with lazy and irresponsible. If I didn't believe you were eventually trainable, I swear I'd fire you."

Flynn didn't glance at the papers. He'd bet bookies odds they were boring. His accountant, on the other hand, both kidnapped and ransomed his interest even when she wasn't breathing hard—and at the moment Molly Weston was breathing smoke. Thoughtfully he scratched his chin. "Don't you think firing me will be a little tricky? Considering that I own the company and you're the employee?"

"If you think that's a relevant argument, you've got another think coming. You're not going to own anything if you don't shape up. You'll be in court with the IRS—and they'd be justified in throwing the book at you. Now, I know you hate numbers, but this is ridiculous. You call these scraps of paper a serious effort at keeping records?"

Truth to tell, he did. Flynn had never needed an accountant when he was poor. Who'd have guessed that his software programs would take off like lightning in the marketplace? For him, the work was fun—pure playtime—or he'd never have done it. The gold he seemed to be hauling in for the last three years was a total accident.

The other three accountants he'd tried before Molly Weston had been total accidents, too. Two guys. One woman. All three of them had quit on him in a disgusted huff, puffing out the door in their pin-stripe suits and their starched spines.

Six months ago, Molly had started out as starched as the rest of them. She'd also started out soft-voiced and sweet and so shy she was intimidated by her own shadow.

Flynn took personal credit for ruining her.

Her pale pink fingertip located a sheet with a bunch of statistics—one of her favorite things in life—and started stabbing it. "You call this a record of expenses? What is this eight hundred dollars for *lunch*?" she snarled at him.

"Well, actually, it wasn't for lunch. It was for that special ergonomic chair for Ralph, because he's got that bad knee? Only I sort of misplaced the receipt, and I knew that'd tick you off, so I thought it'd be easier to..."

"You didn't *think*." She immediately corrected him.

Since he'd heard parts of this harangue before, Flynn cocked his moccasined feet on the desk and concentrated his attention on studying her. She was pacing. To effectively pace in his office, she needed to kick the basketball out of the way and manuever around the putting green by the windows.

Initially Molly had been appalled at the whole place—but especially his office. Personally Flynn thought the plush red carpet, teak cabinets and slab of lapus lazuli desk looked appropriately expensive and executive. Obviously he'd had to add personal touches, like the basketball hoop over the door and the putting green by the far windows. His office chair was almost as good as a mistress—eleven controls, programmed and willing to massage any part of the body on command. It couldn't compete with a woman's hands, but a guy couldn't have everything in a work setting.

Molly wasn't much on vibrating chairs. Her approval rating on his customary working attire of historic jeans and moccasins wasn't much higher. There was no real reason why the staff of five couldn't work stark naked if they chose. Clients came from across the globe, but impromptu visits to the office were rare.

The whole staff, including himself, were creative nerds who holed up in front of their keyboards and worked whatever hours they pleased. Flynn didn't care about any of their life-styles or clothes as long as they did their jobs.

Molly, though, was addicted to formality. She liked suits—preferably navy, black or gray, but on a real wild day she'd go for herringbone. Today she was in Priss Mode. Navy skirt, navy heels, a crisp white blouse with a neat little pin choking her at the collar. Her hair was brownish-gold, the color of rich dark tea, expertly cut just short of her shoulders in a pageboy style. Even when she was pacing around, thwacking papers, threatening his cherished body parts, agitated enough to make her hair tumble and bounce...the instant she paused, her hair fell right back into its customary smooth, silky style. Flynn figured her hair didn't have the nerve to stay mussed.

Her eyes were brown, too, but not tea brown. More melted-chocolate brown. Soft. Emotive. Those huge eyes mirrored her vulnerability, Flynn had always thought. The oval face had more of those hopelessly vulnerable features—feathered brows, delicate cheekbones and an itsy-bitsy mouth that was damn near shaped perfectly—if a man had his mind on kissing her.

Flynn invariably had his mind on kissing her lately. Aw, hell. He had his mind on tussling with her between cool, smooth sheets on a nice, hard mattress. He'd gamble his Lotus she was wearing a good-girl white bra under that crisp linen blouse. He hadn't gotten far enough to find out. Yet.

"Are you listening to me?" she demanded.

"Uh-huh. You want to know why there's extra money in that account. And where the paperwork is to explain where it came from. I'm trying to remember," he assured her.

"You wouldn't *have* to remember if you'd just keep reasonable records from the start! My God, you're as tough to reform as a career criminal. I've set up an entire system to make this easy for you. I know perfectly well that you're deathly allergic to concepts like organization. But I can't help you if you won't even try to come halfway, Flynn."

"Yes, Molly." Even her voice aroused him. There was nothing unique in her accent—they were both immigrants to Kalamazoo, but he'd fled from Detroit and she hailed from Traverse City country, so her speech patterns were as Michigan-based as his. But there was something liquid in her voice tone. Something pure female. Something that went down as easy as honey—even when she was mopping the floor with him.

"I'm serious, you jerk. You're inviting problems with the IRS, and there's no excuse for it. Your business is perfectly sound, for heaven's sake. It isn't that complicated to express that on paper. The rest of the staff has come around like troopers. And then there's you. What exactly is so hard with keeping some simple, basic records?"

"Honestly. I just forget—"

Oops. Forgetting was a mortal sin in her eyes—which you'd think he'd know by now. She was off again, wheeling around his desk, throwing out her right hand, then her left, in gestures to punctuate her lecture about being disgusted with him.

Flynn had been terrified she'd quit like the others—for a while. But Molly claimed quitting would make her feel guilty. If she quit, he'd have to hire someone else. That someone else would be stuck handling his idiocy. As she put it, the buck stopped with her. She was going to shape him up or die trying.

He really *was* trying to shape up, but Molly's standards were rigidly exacting. About work. The two times he'd stolen a kiss from her...well. He hadn't managed to peel off any of those immaculate linen blouses, or find out if that slim, shapely fanny was as sexy as it looked without the zealously prissy skirt. But he'd discovered something fascinating.

Man, could she kiss.

It wasn't Flynn's fault he couldn't forget. She kissed like a man's wildest erotic fantasy. Those lips molded under his as if nature had created that soft, red mouth just for him.

Molly had a bank vault of principles she never bent on.

It wasn't as if she abandoned those values, more like there was a deep emotional current running under those first locked doors.

That current could drag a man under, if he weren't careful. At thirty-four, Flynn had never been caught by the marriage trap, but life would be no fun at all if a man were *too* careful.

"You're not paying attention to me," Molly accused him.

"Believe me, I am. Weston, you have the best set of legs in the Midwest, and probably the whole damn country. And that's an objective opinion from a leg connoisseur."

"McGannon!" The first day he met her, he'd thought scarlet was her natural skin color—she'd been that flushed and nervous through the whole job interview. Now, it took more effort to make a blush bloom on her cheeks, but this was a good one, a full-fledged rose. The blush was old news, but the mischievous sparkle in her eyes was a noticeably gutsy addition.

Ms. Wholesome-Weston definitely wasn't as prim and proper as she used to be. That sparkle in her eyes, in fact, inspired him to swing his legs off the desk.

"No," she said firmly.

"Exactly what are you saying 'no' to?" He stood up.

"Get that look out of your eyes, McGannon. Right now."

He advanced a step. She not only failed to look intimidated, but she also parked two slim fists on her delectably shaped hips. Flynn could still remember how she skittered and jumped if he looked at her crossways in those first days. He'd been bluntly honest with her—she'd never last a week if she couldn't stand up to him. In six months, she'd come a long way.

But not as far as he'd like her to. "You've got the same look in your eyes," he pointed out.

"I do not."

Yeah, she did. And that unholy sparkle in her eyes only upped in wattage when he took another step toward her. And another.

"Back off. Or you'll have a shiner so fast it'll make your head spin, buster."

"Nah. You wouldn't give me a shiner unless I earned it. And there isn't a prayer we'd be doing this if I wasn't sure we both liked it. All you have to do is say no and I'll behave. I swear."

She didn't say no. But when she was backed up against the plush red carpeted wall, she reverted to her favorite defense. Logic. "I like this job and I don't want to lose it."

"That makes two of us. You've made yourself so totally indispensable that I'd be lost with you. I'm not joking. I mean it. I told you the day you hired on that I'm an insensitive clod—but I learn. If I do one thing to make you uncomfortable, all you have to do is say so."

"It's not that simple, and you know it. People comingling where they work is never a good idea. Someone gets hurt, and then someone ends up out of a job."

"It doesn't have to be that way. If both people are honest with each other and play by the same rules."

"You couldn't define 'rule' with a big print dictionary, Flynn. You like anarchy. Everybody doesn't. Some people can't just hop into bed and have everything be the same the next morning."

"Actually I wasn't thinking about hopping into bed. Well, not much anyway. But I do respect that you're real strong on that rings and commitment sort of thing...." He motioned with a hand, indicating his unfamiliarity with those alien concepts. "Really, all I had in mind was a kiss. To see if the last one was some kind of aberration."

"Aberration?"

"Yeah. You put my knickers in the twist the last time we tried this. And I don't wear knickers. Somehow what I assumed would be a little innocent mischief turned into spontaneous combustion. I wasn't expecting it, and to tell you the truth, I hope you won't do it again. You may not believe this, but I've been around a few blocks in life—"

"I believe it."

"—So I'm definitely not used to falling in love on a first kiss. I'm figuring you must have caught me at a weak moment. When my blood sugar was low, or I was catching a fever, something like that. But the thing is, I can't get that last power-punched kiss off my mind. Maybe if we did it again, and the kiss turned out tepid and dull, we could both quit this nonsense and go back to working like normal."

"Flynn…"

Flynn used the word "love" easily, Molly knew. He'd claimed to be in love with her before—her, hot peppers, a crunchy-leaf autumn day, toasted almonds, a staff member who solved a tough problem and any puppy with floppy ears. That was just yesterday. Flynn was an upbeat, boisterously effusive man. "Love" was just a word he used on a daily basis. Molly knew perfectly well he didn't mean it seriously.

But he was standing right in front of her by then. It was a butter-soft fall day, with blinds drawn to shutter out the bright mid-afternoon October sun beating in the windows this early in the afternoon. His computer screen was flashing, his fax noisily spewing out paper, the door to his office wide-open. Molly was aware of the sun, the office textures and noises, yet all she really noticed right then was him.

She was no shrimp at five foot five, yet he towered over her by a good six inches. Flynn always looked more like the wild warriors in his Scottish ancestry than anyone respectably civilized. His eyes were as piercing as blue lasers, his shoulders beam-broad, his thick, unruly hair the color of dark cinnamon and never looked brushed. His clothes were disgraceful the same way—jeans with holes, a long-sleeved black T-shirt with a threadbare neck—the man had money to burn, yet couldn't seem to spare a dime to dress conventionally. Doing anything conventional never seemed to occur to Flynn.

He stood there. Within pouncing distance. But he didn't move—and wouldn't, Molly guessed. Flynn was an unpredictable, amoral, immoral rascal, but he never crossed a certain line. Once she'd made a teasing comment about sexual harassment, and startling her completely, he'd sobered faster than a judge and sat down with her for the next three hours. He'd listened, but Molly could see he honestly didn't get it. That he had power. That he was a boss. He seemed to think of his owning the company as accidental, and unfailingly treated the staff as if they were a team of all equal players, with his vote weighing no more than anyone else's. Flynn's management style didn't fit in any rule book she knew, but sexual harassment never even crossed her mind in a teasing way once she knew him. His code of behavior around women was crystal-clear.

He'd never tried that first kiss, never made any sort of move, until she'd invited it. He never intruded anywhere near a woman's principles or choices.

Unless she were willing.

And let him know she was willing.

Those damn blue eyes of his were waiting. A kiss simmered between them like an untasted stew, the scent tantalizing, the hunger aroused by the possibilities.

Molly mused that she'd heard him call himself homely once.

Possibly he even believed it—heaven knew, his clothes reflected a total blindness or lack of perception about his physical appearance. Technically the blunt chin and craggy nose and broad-planed bones fit no classic claim to handsomeness...but he was still the sexiest man she knew. Those blue eyes could caress a woman before he'd even touched her; the mouth could tempt a nun to jettison her vows and jump him. The problem with Flynn—one of many—was that he loved everything about being a man, and it showed. He couldn't seem to help being dangerous. That compelling, earthy sexuality was downright impossible to ignore, and God knew, she'd tried.

"You stalling, Ms. Weston?" he murmured.

"Yes."

"You thinking about it? Whether you want me to kiss you or whether you want to knock my block off?"

"Yes."

"Are you going to let me know before November what you decide?"

Maybe she needed that whole month, Molly thought desperately. Her decision should have been cut and dried, but somehow it wasn't. Six months ago, if anyone suggested she could conceivably fall in love with a man like Flynn McGannon, she'd have checked herself into a funny farm for immediate shock treatments.

He was a bellower. A man who expressed both humor and temper at the same roaring volume. He worked like a slave, played like a glutton, intimidated strangers and clients both with his booming voice and unpredictable moods—and then invariably acted confounded why anybody would be afraid of him.

Molly knew precisely why she was.

He was too sexy for her. Too sexy, too self-centered, too dare-the-world wild, too everything that she wasn't. She wanted a husband, children, a family. Not an affair with a man who was bluntly honest about his terror of wedding rings. Flynn loved risk. She honestly hated it. He saw every day as a free-wheeling adventure. She was a list-maker.

Nothing could come from kissing him but trouble. Heartache. A woman as sane as she was—and the whole world knew Molly Weston was practical and hopelessly straitlaced—simply had more brains than to hurl herself off a cliff without a parachute.

But he tempted her. Like no man ever had. It was those eyes. It was that nasty, simmering, electric thing that shimmered in the air between them. It was that daredevil zest for life that captivated her, and made crazy ideas fester in her mind—like that she'd regret it forever if she never made love with him. Like that she might only have this one chance. Like that maybe everyone should have the right, just once in life, to do something foolish and impulsive....

She heard sudden commotion from outside his office. A door slamming. Voices raised. Pandemonium wasn't uncommon in the workday at McGannon's, but something registered in her mind as off-kilter. Still, she couldn't look away from the heat in Flynn's gaze. Didn't want to.

He wanted her. Maybe Flynn desired a couple hundred women—possibly even in the same day—but the whole sensation was new to Molly. She'd never felt washed in the warm liquid gaze of a man's desire, bold, nakedly honest, dangerous, magnetic. She'd never figured out how the patooties she'd ever stirred his interest. Most men pegged her accurately and swiftly—she was a conventional woman, a picture-straightener, an obsessive list-maker, attractive enough but in a *nice* way. Everyone knew she was nice, for Pete's sake. It was probably going to be on her epitaph.

Not him. He looked at her like she was Christie Brinkley who'd just popped in to strip for him. Or like she was a succulent choice bit of lobster and he'd just come off a week's fast. She knew that was all nuts—but something went haywire in her perceptions around Flynn. Never mind what was real. How he made her feel was painfully real enough.

She'd been falling in love with him for months now. Denying it. Making excuses—calling it hormones, calling it PMS, calling it an affection that had naturally developed from working with a fascinating man every day. She'd been calling it every word under the sun but the one she was afraid was true.

Her hand lifted. Fingers already curving to the shape of his neck.

He saw. That slow, wicked grin of his faded. His face almost turned grave—and Flynn rarely took anything in life too seriously. His gaze shifted from her eyes to her mouth, the playfulness disappearing from his expression. This kiss would be different, she sensed.

The other ones really hadn't been without a parachute. But this one might be.

Still her hand raised higher, until her fingers were bare, naked inches from touching him. Her heart was suddenly pounding, pounding.

Until she heard the bellowing wail of a baby.

Molly stepped back, startled, just as a woman barreled into Flynn's office. And not just a woman, but a baby—

a pumpkin-shaped squirt of maybe a year old, who was squirming in every direction and announcing loudly to the world that he was unhappy. The woman was flustered and distraught, trying to juggle the eel of a baby and baby gear and a flapping purse.

"Flynn, damn you. No one wanted to even let me see you...I practically had to battle past a nutcase in a bathrobe at the front desk—"

Molly froze for a second. Flynn whirled around. Bailey shot in just behind the woman, his face flushed like a brick—and yes, he was wearing a bathrobe over his clothes. Bailey was one of Flynn's brilliant creative nerds; very sweet, just a little goofy. When he had a creative challenge inspiring him, he wore his lucky robe. No one paid attention, not even Molly anymore. Bailey never voluntarily met the public, because nerves brought out his stutter—and he was stuttering painfully, trying to explain to Flynn how the lady had barged past him.

Molly heard that conversation, but she wasn't really listening. The intrusion was just so bizarre.

The woman dropped a diaper bag on the carpet. Then she plunked down the baby with the same kind of exasperated attitude. The baby, let free, quit bellowing and squirming and promptly took off on all fours.

"What on earth...?" Flynn reached behind him to yank the blinds open further. Cheerful sunlight instantly poured in, but didn't seem to illuminate anything that was going on. Flynn wasn't easily thrown by any brand or flavor of surprises. His bushy eyebrows lifted in question, but initially his expression showed more intrigue than concern over the mystery woman's arrival.

Molly didn't catch the lady's face until she straightened back up. Golden hair billowed around her shoulders then. A red sweater hugged a top-heavy bust; poured-on jeans showed off several miles of slim legs. Her face might have been strikingly pretty, if there hadn't been huge shadows under the eyes and drawn lines around the mouth.

"Don't you 'What on earth' me, Flynn McGannon. And don't even try claiming not to recognize me." Either fury or nerves made her voice shrill. Molly could see the skilled effort with makeup, but it didn't conceal the pallor of her skin or the exhausted dark eyes.

"I didn't claim anything. But I honestly don't know…" Flynn was frowning now, studying her hard.

"Virginie," she snapped. "Tuscon. The Silver Buckle. Add up thirteen months—the age of your son—and the nine months I carried him, and maybe that night'll come back to you. You were with some party. I was with some party. But the only party that mattered was the one that ended up back at my place. Chivas was your drink that night, as I recall. Unfortunately, I recall more than that. You were a hell of a lover, you cretin. But no man's worth the price you cost me."

"Son?" Flynn echoed blankly, and then wildly shook his head. "That isn't possible. You said you were protected—"

"Ha. So suddenly you *do* remember that night—and if it isn't just like a man to remember the part that gives him an excuse. And at the time, I was. On the pill. But I missed a couple—and before you tell me that was my fault, let me tell you that I don't give a damn. That doesn't make the baby any less your responsibility—"

"Look, if you'd just try to calm down…you can't just show up out of the blue, making claims that you seem to expect me to instantly believe—"

Virginie didn't try responding to that. She seemed on a one-track road, the words spilling out of her at cyclone speed. "Your son's name is Dylan. And he's all yours as of this minute. You don't know what I've been through. You can't even guess. My life's been a nonstop nightmare from the instant this child was conceived. I was sick. Lost my job. He had colic and he doesn't sleep and I'm about to lose my apartment and I can't do it anymore. Right now I don't even have a way to feed him—"

"Wait a minute. *Wait* a minute, just slow down—"

"The hell I will. And don't waste your breath offering me money because this isn't about money. It's about everything. I never figured you'd want to know you were a father, but that's just tough. Every woman on earth isn't cut out for motherhood. I gave it a shot—you don't know how hard I gave it a shot—but nothing's working out. I can't do it anymore, and you're responsible for this. It took me forever to find you—"

Molly had never seen Flynn lose color before. Normally when he was upset, he got noisy, not quiet. But he raked a hand through his hair and looked dead-quiet now. "Surely you realize this is impossible? You can't just barge in here and claim I'm the father of a child. I can see you're upset, but if you'd just calm down—"

"I'm not calming down. I'm leaving. You. With your son."

"It's *not* my son." Flynn's baritone could have carried to the next county. So could the blonde's shrill soprano.

"Oh, yeah it is. I know it is. And if you'll look back twenty-one months ago, you'll know it is. If not, there has to be some blood test or something that'll prove it to you—because believe me, it will." She snatched up her tote-size purse again, but withdrew a folder from it and tossed it on his desk. Pictures spilled out. What looked like medical records, maybe a birth certificate. "I need a job. I need a place to live. I need a chance at life again, and I'm going after it. The baby ruined everything I ever had. He's your problem from this minute on."

When she spun around, Flynn lurched toward her. "Wait a minute. For God's sake, you can't just walk out of here—"

"Watch me."

Molly couldn't seem to unfreeze. The whole scene was just so unreal. The frantic-faced woman and the whole yelling match couldn't have taken five minutes. She stormed back out of the office as fast as she'd stormed in.

Flynn hiked after her. Molly had never seen his complexion turn that ashen gray before. She heard his booming voice from the hall, fading as the two of them reached the front doors. There wasn't another sound in the entire office—not because Flynn's handful of staff weren't there, but likely because everyone had been listening as intently to the whole scene no differently than she had.

It took a few seconds before Molly could seem to gather her wits. And another second before she abruptly realized that the infamous "Virginie" had left a package behind her.

The baby had been padding around on all fours, fanny in the air, crawling at cruising speeds that could probably earn him a ticket on the freeway.

Temporarily, though, the baby was nowhere in sight.

And no one seemed to give a damn.

TWO

Molly hustled out of Flynn's office in search of the baby.

Initially real worry never occurred to her—she figured she'd have heard the sound of the baby crying if he'd been in trouble, and there were other adults around besides. She just wanted to find him. It wasn't the safest environment in town for a crawling toddler to be running around loose.

Flynn's office opened into the circular area that the staff called Brainstorming Central. Undoubtedly the original architect had designed a normal office space with walls and doors, but Flynn had predictably obliterated all that logical construction long since.

The virtual reality booth was an intrinsic part of the "think tank," but she poked her head in there—and found no baby. In the middle of Brainstorming Central was a table the size of a small country. Recliner chairs tipped back as far as beds. The ceiling was lavishly decorated with posters—cartoon characters, wilderness scenes, rock stars, bad jokes, saintly inspirational quotes. Molly first thought that decorating the ceiling was loony, but after six months of working with the lunatic staff, she'd discovered she was too fond of all of them to take exception to their eccentric office decor ideas.

She whipped around the circumference of the table, bent over to spot any miniature bodies, checking chairs and any possible hiding spot. Still, she caught no sight or sound of the mite.

Her pulse was charging, her heart clanging nerves. She told herself she was naturally concerned about the missing Dylan, but that was only a partial truth. She'd been rattled long before realizing the baby had disappeared. The whole bizarre scene with Dylan's mother had acid jumping in her stomach...and worse than that, her mind kept doing instant replays of the embrace she'd almost invited from Flynn.

A lump clogged her throat as she sprinted out of Brainstorming Central toward the break rooms. All right. Embrace was a pale word for what she'd been inviting from Flynn. She'd wanted to make love with him. Could have, might have, wanted to—if they hadn't been interrupted at that precise moment.

Thoughts spun in her mind like whirling dervishes in a high wind. Darn it, was that baby really his? And had Flynn really slept with that woman—a woman he barely seemed to recognize?

Molly had been so positive she knew him. His impulsiveness and unpredictability were part of what made him an exciting, dynamic man, and yes, those character traits made her uneasy, too. Maybe he was wild, but she'd never known him to do anything seriously irresponsible. She'd believed he had a good heart. And now...

Now you aren't sure of anything, duckie. Except that there's a baby loose and someone has to find the little one before he gets hurt.

She flipped the light switch in the bathroom and peered in—no baby. She closed that door and charged into the first break room. Since none of Flynn's staff—besides herself—had even a remote concept of normal work hours, the back room contained bunk beds, a stereo and TV entertainment center. It wasn't unusual to find someone crashing in there any hour of the day, but Molly peered under beds and around corners and closets. No bodies surfaced, large or small.

Still, those whirling-dervish thoughts kept hurling through her mind. Had he really had a one-night stand with someone he didn't know, didn't value, just a fling between the sheets to satisfy an itch—was that all sex meant to Flynn? And yeah, Molly knew she was just a teensy bit rigid…aw hell, her dad used to say she'd strangle on a principle before giving an inch, but that didn't stop the sick-dread feeling from churning in her stomach. All the times Flynn had playfully tried to seduce her, she'd thought she was special to him. She'd thought they were building something special between them. She'd really thought…

Quit thinking, you dimwit. Find the baby.

She pedaled into the second break room, and immediately spotted a body—just not the size body she was searching for.

Like everyone else at McGannon's, Simone Akumi was a character. She was Flynn's chief programmer, and stood a regal six feet, with a face the color of dark mahogany and austere features that reflected her personality. Her IQ scored off the map, but she had a tough time talking to lesser mortals. Typically she was garbed in a long, flowing

African print—with a headset parked on her wiry white hair. The headset meant she was working, and only someone with a death wish interrupted Simone when she was concentrating. Molly rapidly scanned the room before trying to catch her attention.

Glass doors led outside to a patio and rolling sweep of lawn—Flynn had been known to have staff meetings picnic-style on the grass. But on a crisp October day, thankfully the doors were safely closed, so the baby couldn't escape that way. Past the counter table was a double-size refrigerator—anything could be in there, from mystery meat to sushi to pizza to a quart jar of maraschino cherries. Three coffeemakers were simultaneously bubbling on the sink counter. Everyone was violently fussy—and possessive—about their favorite brands. Simone just turned around to pour a mug when Molly frantically motioned for her to lift one ear cup.

"Did you see it? A baby anywhere around here?"

"If you're referring to that small hellion of a Caucasian traveling on all fours—good Lord, is it really Flynn's?" Simone, for once, didn't seem to mind the interruption.

But Molly had no time to chat. "I don't know. I just know it disappeared when everyone was talking—"

"Well, the last I saw it, it was trailing after Bailey. Poor tyke. Clearly it's too young to have developed any sort of judgment in people. And Bailey looked petrified." Simone adjusted her headphones back in place. From her expression, she was back to concentrating on work before Molly had even spun around.

With her heart thudding, she clipped double-speed into the work area shared by all the programmers. Maybe she hadn't been really that worried about the baby before, but darn it, Bailey was even more absentminded than Simone, and the programming office was the most dangerous place for a little one. Computers and printers and modems created an incessant nerve-racking clatter. Phones and cords and all kinds of electronic equipment were too easily reachable by small fingers.

Ralph's cubicle was first—and he was there, ensconced in his orange throne chair that wincingly clashed with the red carpet. He was twenty-four, typically working barefoot, with a plaid shirt buttoned nerd-style to the throat, and a long, straggly blond ponytail swinging behind him. He was pounding at two keyboards—pretty much simultaneously—and since Ralph wouldn't likely notice a tornado when he was working, there was little point in grilling him.

She pelted past his work cubicle, then past Simone's and Darren's—Darren was working at home today—then barreled around the corner to Bailey's. She stopped dead, her hand pressing tight to her heaving heart.

The search was over.

Bailey was on all fours, his balding head shining under the fluorescent light. Bailey might be goofy enough to wear a "lucky bathrobe" over a pin-striped shirt, but he was a brilliant man. People skills weren't exactly his strength, but he was inspired by impossible problems, attacked every challenge with the same dour, methodical, pedantic perseverance. Molly saw his hind end before she spotted the baby. Bailey, grave as a judge, seemed to have attacked this particular problem by cornering it under his desk. Guessing from the sea of wadded-up paper littering the floor, the two of them had been playing ball.

"Bailey, for Pete's sake, I've been looking everywhere for the baby—" A breath that felt as if she must have been holding it for five solid minutes whooshed out of her lungs.

"Sheesh, it's about time someone came in and saved me." Bailey, sounding pitifully aggrieved, scooched away from the baby as soon as he spotted her. "I've been having a heart attack. It crawled in here after me and then it let out this wail loud enough to curdle milk. How was I supposed to know what it wanted? I never had any kids! Flynn ran out after that woman, and I didn't know where you were, and I didn't know what I was supposed to do—"

"Bailey, you turkey! I don't know anything about children, either, but I can't believe you sat right there and let the baby eat *paper!*"

"Let? Let? Like I had some choice in the matter? The first thing the child did was grab some paper and start chewing. *You* try taking it away from him and see what happens."

"He cries, huh?"

Bailey was more explicit. "The kid has a set of lungs like a hyena."

Molly crouched down. The little one had a giant mouthful of paper and was extremely busy, trying to stuff in more. She obviously had to get the paper away from him, but for one stark second, she felt an emotional fist squeeze her heart tight. The scene in Flynn's office had happened so fast and furiously that she really hadn't caught a good look at Dylan before.

The baby had a pudgy little body and chunky legs and, oh my, a terribly homely face. The chin of a prizefighter in miniature, plain bones, a bump of a nose—Dylan just wasn't going to be auditioning for the Gerber poster child, but Molly told herself maybe he could grow into all that character potential. That wasn't, though, the reason her heart stopped.

The little one had exuberant bristles of auburn hair. The

color of Flynn's. Exactly the color of Flynn's. And maybe the baby was no beauty, but the eyes…the eyes were cerulean sky blue, as bright and full of light—and mischief—as Flynn's.

Molly's heart just seemed to freeze. She really hadn't wanted to believe the woman in his office. Virginie had obviously been distraught, irrational, terribly beside herself. Hardly a credible source. But the look of Dylan cast a different color on things. There was no ignoring that the likeness between the two did exist.

The baby acknowledged her closeness by lifting those heart-throbber blue eyes to her face.

"Hi there, sweetie. Dylan…"

"You're going to take him out of here, aren't you?" Bailey said nervously.

"If he'll let me pick him up. But I'm not going to do anything fast and scare him. For heaven's sake, he doesn't know me, do you, love bug?" She kept her voice low and soft, and tried a smile. The urchin smiled back, revealing two brilliant white teeth—and a mouth chockful of drool-coated paper. "I don't suppose you'd let me reach in there and take out that paper, would you?"

The smile vanished. The baby's lips clamped closed faster than a vault at Fort Knox.

"Okay, okay, we'll forget about that for a second or two. Would you like to come with me for a bit? I'll show you my office. It's the only normal spot in the whole place. And maybe we could come up with a cracker from the kitchen. Dylan go with Molly?"

"Dylan go with Molly," Bailey parroted urgently.

Dylan grinned at Molly, grinned at Bailey, and then whipped his fanny in the air and took off on all fours in the opposite direction.

Molly had the fleeting thought that she only knew one other male on the planet with that kind of contrary nature.

And then she chased after the miniature redhead.

Less than a half hour passed before Molly heard knuckles rap on her office door. Sooner or later she figured Flynn would track her down—and the whereabouts of the baby. The question was just how long he was tied up talking with the child's mother...or trying to talk with her. Molly was sitting behind her desk when Flynn turned the knob and poked his head in.

"Simone said the baby was with you?"

"Yup, safe and sound." Or her office had seemed safe and sound until Flynn stepped in, Molly thought dryly. She'd only closed the door to keep the baby contained. Unlike all the other offices at McGannon's, hers was a haven of normalcy. A traditional desk. File cabinets. Two sturdy chairs. Pencils sharpened to uniform points were neatly aligned in a Monet mug; a photo of her parents and two younger sisters sat on the credenza; the files on her desk were color-coded and stacked as straight as a ruler.

The orderly, tidy atmosphere changed irrevocably the instant Flynn arrived. It always did. Molly was never quite sure how he could turn a nice, quiet, peaceful day into a tornado of testosterone. The sizzle in the atmosphere was always a sudden thing, like the first crack of lightning before a storm. One instant she was a CPA, the next, she was aware of her breasts and hips, whether her hair might be messy, what she'd look like to him naked. Molly had tried to analyze the problem from a dozen different angles, but there seemed no answers—except that Flynn had the unnerving gift for making a woman feel restless. Edgy. Alive, as if someone had tickled her awake from a sound sleep.

Momentarily, though, he was the edgy one. "She's gone," he said. "I still can't believe it. Nothing I said to her made any difference. She took off. Just like that."

Molly leaned back in her office chair, watching him pace. "I was afraid she would. When she walked out of your office, she didn't seem to be listening to anyone about anything. But I'm sure she'll be back, Flynn. She was just terribly upset. No mother would just desert her baby like that."

"Well, I assume she'll be back, too. But damned if I know what I'm supposed to do in the meantime. I feel like somebody dropped a bomb in my lap—what if the kid got sick, right now, right this minute? Who's responsible for it? I don't even know if I have the legal right to get care for it—for God's sake, I don't even believe the child is mine."

Molly wasn't sure what Flynn believed. He was thrown for six. That was obvious. But she couldn't help but be aware that he hadn't really looked at the baby—not earlier, when Virginie had staged that scene, and not now.

Dylan was safe enough. Molly had scooped up his diaper bag from the office, a blanket from the break room, crackers and a mug of milk from the kitchen—the cracker had been bribery to con the baby into giving up his mouthful of paper. The urchin had charged around her office for a couple of minutes on all fours, and then simply curled up on the blanket...one minute a dynamo of energy, the next snoozing harder than a whipped puppy.

Flynn had to realize the baby was right there. No matter how agitatedly he was pacing around, he never even accidentally came close to that blanket. Now, though, he punched a fist into his palm. "There are things I obviously have to do immediately. Call a lawyer, for one. And find out what pediatricians are in town. And maybe I should be calling my doc, too…hell, I don't know what kind of tests are done to prove or disprove parentage…"

"Flynn?"

"What?" He stopped hurling himself around the office long enough to look at her. She'd had some time separate from him—time to get tough, to firm up her common sense, to put any unmanageable emotions on chill until she was ready to handle them. But it was still rough seeing that devastated look in Flynn's eyes. God knew, he responded to everything volatilely and emotionally—but nothing like this. Even if he'd brought every ounce of the problem on himself, he'd still never had that drawn white look around his eyes before.

"I think you're right…that you need to do all those things," she said quietly. "But I'm afraid you have a more critical priority than any of that."

His eyebrows lifted in query. "Like what?"

"Like the baby himself, McGannon. He needs food. More diapers than were in that bag. A crib, or something to sleep in. And she put some clothes in there, but not enough to last more than a few days."

"Molly…" Flynn threw himself in the chair opposite her desk, and focused on her with those incredibly electric blue eyes. "I can't do any of that stuff. I've never been around a baby, wouldn't have a clue what to buy or what it needs—"

"Neither have I. *No,* Flynn."

"No? I didn't ask you anything."

"But you were going to. I took on the baby for a few minutes because someone had to—and I was glad to help. But just because I'm a female doesn't make me a born expert in child care. I haven't been around little ones, either. I honestly don't know any more than you do."

"You *have* to know more than I do," Flynn muttered,

and yanked a hand through his scalp. "A stone would know more than I do about babies. A leaf. A slab of concrete. I've got work on my desk higher than a mountain, a project halfway done, the phone's ringing…I don't even know how to suddenly stop an entire business for a child—"

"Flynn," she said gently, firmly. "Look at him."

But he wouldn't look at the child. He just kept looking at her, with those eyes as magnetic as blue lightning. There was so much power and character in his face, more natural charisma than one man had a right to. But it was the honesty of anxiety in his expression that touched her far more now. "This isn't your problem, Molly, I realize that," he said slowly. "But I don't know who else to ask for help. Not until I at least figure out what I'm supposed to do with him."

Molly sighed. She really couldn't imagine Bailey or Simone pinch-hitting. Not with a problem like this. "Well, he's sleeping now. And I realize you really do need to make those phone calls and get some business squared away. He can stay here until he wakes up."

Flynn didn't move. Just kept looking at her with that confounded helpless expression—until Molly threw up her hands in exasperation.

"All right, all right. After that I'll go shopping with you. I realize that'd be really hard for you to do alone, and with a baby in tow besides. But I'm warning you ahead, my advice is worthless. I don't know anything! The best I can say is that between two adult heads, we should be able to handle picking out at least some basic baby supplies."

Well, darn it, she thought. That was what she thought he wanted—her offering help. Yet once she suckered in that far, he still didn't look happy. Flynn invariably bellowed and barreled into most tricky life situations, but he still hadn't budged, and his voice turned bass-low and careful.

"You're angry with me, aren't you. You're not looking at me the same way, talking to me the same way. She really upset you."

"Maybe you'd better call her Virginie instead of 'she.' If she's the mother of your child, I think it might be appropriate for you to remember her name."

"I'm not a father," he said quietly, clearly.

"Look at the baby," she said again.

But he didn't. "No matter what she said...no matter what you think...I've never been careless with a woman. Not once. Not ever. There are reasons why I've stayed unattached, reasons why I never wanted to be a father. I'm not saying I've been a saint, Molly, but I never knowingly risked a child. I'm asking you to believe me."

Molly fussed with her pencils on the desk. "Actually she blurted out rather clearly that she'd skipped some birth control pills—"

"I heard what she said. I heard every damn word she said. But that has nothing to do with your believing me."

"McGannon..." Molly felt all tangled up, unsure what was so important to him, what he wanted her to say. "Look, trying to talk right now is nuts. You need to scoot. I don't have a clue how long a baby naps, but every minute is borrowed time. Get whatever business cleared away that you can."

He seemed inclined to argue—but didn't. Once he peeled out of that chair and left, Molly pressed two fingers to her temples, her gaze instinctively honing on the sleeping baby.

She'd seen Flynn thrown plenty of times. He ranted and raved as a life-style, but that was just because he was boisterously emotional by nature. At a gut level, he thrived on challenges. The more impossible the problem, the more it revved his personal engines.

But not this one. Any man would be shook up to have a baby suddenly thrown into his life, Molly realized, but Flynn…there was something more. His face had gone cold, his voice stone-harsh when he'd said there were reasons why he never wanted to be a father. Something painful had to be behind that. She wished she knew what. The damn man could flirt all day and then some…but Flynn never revealed anything personal about himself, had never admitted anything painful to her before. For Flynn to express that kind of gut honesty was a vulnerable measure that he was seriously shook up.

But so was she. Shook up—from the inside out. Her pulse was still rattling. She'd been falling hard and deep for him—painfully hard, dangerously deeply. And she had no idea before that moment that Flynn was stone-set against being a father. How could she love a man who didn't want children, didn't love babies, couldn't even look at that adorable homely face snoozing on the carpet?

She didn't know him. The echo bleated in her soul. He'd bamboozled her hormones…and yes, she'd known he was wild and impulsive and full of the devil. The charm that made him downright irresistible as a lover never meant he was serious husband material. But she'd still never imagined that Flynn would pick up a strange woman for a one-night stand…that maybe he'd seduced dozens of women the same way he turned the charm on her. Making love to him would have been a land mine for Molly. For Flynn, sex could just be another three-letter word like fun.

And in the meantime, there seemed to be a snoozing baby on her carpet that no one seemed to love—or want.

Molly could too easily see herself getting roped into care-taking the little one. She recognized that Flynn honestly needed some help—some immediate help—but he had to have family, she told herself. Friends. Someone. She couldn't let this be her problem.

Her heart went out to the child.

But only for the baby's sake. Not for Flynn's.

Three

"Flynn, that diaper package says Newborn. I think you need a size for a much bigger baby."

"You mean diapers come in different sizes? Oh. Oh, my God. You have to be kidding me. This is almost as intimidating as the aisle with the women's stockings and trying to figure out what all those egg shapes mean." However pitiful his joke, it earned him a roll of the eyes from Molly. They were making progress, Flynn thought. At least she was speaking to him again—even if the atmospheric temperature between them still hovered between freezing and subzero. "So, what'd you think? Toddler size?"

"That'd be my best guess."

"Okeydoke." He scooped up all the toddler-size diaper packages on the shelf and dumped them into the cart. Darned if that didn't win him an outright chuckle.

"McGannon, you nut, you've cleaned out their entire

supply! You really think the baby needs quite that many?''

"Listen, Mol, as far as I can tell, this kid's a leaker. Put anything in one end, and thirty seconds later it comes out the other. I'm not risking running out in the middle of the night…what's next on your list?''

"Food.'' Predictably Molly had a systematic list in one hand, a sharpened pencil in the other. "I'm not sure what to buy. Milk and cereal-type things are pretty obvious, but I think he only has two teeth. Whatever we get, it needs to be food that he doesn't have to chew.''

"Marshmallows,'' Flynn suggested.

"I had in mind something more nutritious,'' she said dryly.

"Well, yeah. But marshmallows are a staple of life. And how about hot chocolate? That's a good kid thing, isn't it?''

"I'll tell you what. You find the baby food aisle and I'll take care of making the choices. And Flynn, for Pete's sake! Take your keys out of the baby's mouth!''

"You can't be serious. You heard him when we walked in here. Until I gave him the keys, I thought he was dying. I thought someone was stabbing him in the back with a knife. I thought we were gonna be arrested for noise pollution—''

"I believe he was trying to clearly communicate that he was slightly bored. I also believe it's possible that Dylan inherited that bellow from his father's side of the family…but we won't go into that again. I don't think your keys are a good play toy—they aren't clean.''

"Not clean? On what planet is that supposed to be relevant? You're talking about a kid who tries to pig out on paper and carpet lint.''

"You think he's getting hungry? We're not even halfway through this list, and darn it! I didn't even think of a car seat." She started scribbling again. "You *have* to have a car seat for a baby this size. It's the law."

"Mol?"

"Hmm?" She was almost too busy penciling stuff on her list to look up.

"Thanks," he said quietly. "For coming with me. I know I've been making jokes, but I don't want you to think I don't seriously appreciate your helping me out."

For a few seconds the ice chips seemed to melt in her eyes.

He caught a glimmer of a spring thaw...but it didn't last. "You'd better wait until we're done before you thank me. When you write out the check for this, you may have a stroke."

Holy kamoly, she filled four carts before calling it quits.

Naturally Flynn had experienced the inside of a grocery store before, but never with a shopping pro. Molly zipped and zoomed down the aisles, checking things off her list, cooing to the baby and muttering about prices at the same time.

Flynn didn't have a stroke about the amount of the check, but a full-fledged panic attack hit him when they reached the parking lot.

Night had fallen faster than a stone, temperatures dropping just as swiftly. His black Lotus had a thimble-size trunk space. There wasn't a prayer of stuffing all the baby loot into his car. Her more sensible Taurus was parked next to his, gleaming white under the parking lot neon lights. Molly's face looked pearl-soft in the evening shadows, but her stockinged legs and suit jacket were inadequate protection against that crisp, sharp air and she was starting to shiver.

She was also busy. As if she didn't trust him, she took

charge of Dylan, and was organizing the baby in the car seat as if she were a general attacking a strategic logistics problem. "I don't think baby car seats are meant for sports cars, but I do believe he's finally secure..."

Finally she lifted her head. Finally—for the first time since this whole blasted store outing began—her eyes met his, but her gaze shifted away faster than the spin of a dime. "Getting all this stuff to your place, though, is another problem entirely. Unless you've got another suggestion, I don't see we have another choice...we're just going to have to fill my trunk, and then I'll follow you to your place."

"I hate to ask you to do that," Flynn said, which had to be the biggest lie he'd told in a year.

"There just is no other way. But you'd better give me your address in case I lose you in traffic."

Like a kid scared when the lights were turned off, he didn't want Molly to leave him. The feeling of dependence was totally alien. He'd grown up stubborn, sweating out his fears of the dark alone, working his way through school, never asking for anything from anyone. Given his background, he'd learned young to count on no one but himself, but that kind of pride and independence had dominated his whole life.

Not now. Not tonight. At the moment he had the pride of a wilted turnip. He watched Molly's headlights in the rearview mirror, checking every few seconds to make sure he hadn't lost her on the whole drive to his place. Once past the traffic on Westnedge, the cars thinned out. For the last half mile, suburban busyness disappeared altogether and the only lights on the road belonged to the two of them.

Flynn wasn't anxiety-prone. He liked chaos. Hell, he'd practically built chaos into a life-style—and was damn content with his choice. But his heart had been beating to panicked drums ever since Virginie blew into his office that afternoon.

He hadn't stopped moving since then. He'd needed a couple of hours on the phone—to call his lawyer, to call his doctor about blood tests, and to start checking the pediatricians in town for credentials. But he barely got started on any of that before Molly showed up in his office doorway with the caterwauling minisize redhead.

His mind should have been on Dylan. And was. The problem of the baby loomed like a cyclone on his emotional horizon, but damnation, Molly was a cyclone-size problem, too. Even after intensively working together for the last six months, he couldn't explain what she'd come to mean to him. He knew she was the marrying kind, that flirting too far with her was dangerous…he also knew that he'd been daring her, daring himself, daring the two of them toward a cliff edge of risk that wasn't wise.

Flynn had never overvalued wisdom. He valued…life. Every day had the intrinsic capacity for adventure. There was an excitement in air, food, water—anything, everything—but only if a guy looked, only if he opened his life to risk and all the possibilities.

Maybe he and Molly were temperamentally chalk and cheese. But he'd had her regard before this. She'd liked him, he knew. She'd found something in him to respect. It went beyond hormones, beyond that nice, hot, sexual attraction firing between them with both barrels.

At least until Virginie blew into his office that afternoon.

Flynn pulled into his driveway. On cue, as he turned the key, the sidekick in the car seat next to him let out a pithy squawl. He whipped his head around. Yeah, Molly was still there, pulling up behind him. His heart could postpone that panic attack for a little while longer.

Molly popped her trunk, then stepped out of her car and took a quick, cool drink of the view. Humor flashed in her eyes as she hiked past him toward the baby. "Honestly, McGannon. I could have guessed this was your house even if I hadn't seen the address."

"How so?"

"It's a castle."

"A castle? Actually it's pretty small—"

"Size has nothing to do with it. Only a creative-type dreamer would be drawn to this place."

"You don't like it?" Flynn had imagined bringing her here a dozen times.

"Oh, I like it—but I'm just chuckling because of how uniquely it suits you. And I hear our rock-star-in-training revving up the volume. I'll get Dylan, if you just unlock the front door and start hauling things in."

Flynn suspected she was subtly trying to suggest that he quit standing there like a dead stick. And while she unthreaded the baby from the car seat torture device, he swiftly fished into his pocket for the door key. Still, as he heaped his arms with bags to carry in, he glanced at his house.

The place was no castle. It was just old. And Molly's dreamer label miffed him. Maybe he'd impulsively fallen in love and bought the property on sight, but it had taken months of elbow grease—not dreams—to make the old white elephant livable. The core structure was stone, with a tall, shake-shingle roof and old-fashioned mullioned windows that reflected silver in the moonlight. But a gabled roof and some skinny mullioned windows hardly made it look like some prissy girl *castle*.

Flynn opened the double front doors, elbowed in with

his packages and quickly flicked on an overhead light. Molly jogged in behind him with the baby. "Maybe you'll like it more when you see the inside," he said defensively. "I had to have some space. I'd get claustrophobic in a city-type apartment. There's woods out the back, and a creek. And I do a lot of work at home, so I had to renovate some things on the inside—"

"I can see." She was busy juggling The Squirmer, but not so busy that she didn't shoot a look around inside. Again, her eyes danced with dry humor. "I wasn't criticizing you, Flynn. It's a romantic house. Ideal for an unconventional dreamer."

"I'm *not* a romantic."

"Oops. Did I touch a nerve? I'll be careful not to use any dirty words like 'romantic' again…the baby's fussing. I think you'd better bring in the diapers first."

He brought in the diapers—and all the other confounded stuff, heaping it all in the stone foyer just inside the door. On those in-and-out treks, he either caught glimpses of Molly or heard her, talking to the baby, using her nice, warm, sexy-as-sin sensual voice—not like the one she'd been using with him all afternoon.

And somehow he'd counted on her liking his place. *He* did. Hell, everything was perfect—at least for a guy living alone. He'd put barn beams and a skylight in the great room, bought three giant forest green couches and elled them around the man-size stone fireplace. He wasn't much on pictures and doodads, but the media entertainment center was prime. A thick, fat white alpaca rug made a great place to lay by a roaring fire on a blizzardy night.

As he peeled off his jacket, the goods all carried in, he thought Molly'd look damn near outstanding on that white alpaca rug. Naked. Well, maybe still wearing stockings...if he was going to fantasize, he might as well go whole hog.

The fantasy died a fast death when she stepped through the arched doorway of the kitchen, still holding the baby. "Are you done bringing everything in?"

Her voice was cool enough to chill champagne. "Yeah. Everything's out of both cars...but after all your help and the trouble I've put you through, I'd like to treat you to dinner."

"Thanks, but I'd better be going. That's quite a kitchen you've got in there. Every labor-saving appliance known to man and woman both."

"You didn't like the kitchen, either?"

"McGannon, you seem to think I'm on your case. You have a fantastic house, ultracool. Every inch of it suits you."

"You haven't seen the upstairs. I could give you a quick tour."

"Maybe another time. Here you go." She lifted Dylan and plopped the wriggling chunk into his arms. "I changed his diaper, and I put out some toddler baby food on the counter. The directions said you could microwave it but you'll need to be careful it's not too hot."

She was trotting for the front door faster than a filly in a sulky race. "You're sure you won't stay for dinner—?"

"Positive." She opened the front door.

"Molly, wait." Dylan whacked him on the ear with a baby fist. Flynn heard alarm bells of anxiety clanging in his ears—and not just because the baby had given him a boxer's whack. "I appreciate your helping me out. I owe you a big thanks."

"No sweat. You're welcome."

Flynn let the baby down, since there was no holding

on to the contortionist anyway. Dylan immediately quit squawking, plunked down on all fours and took off again. Molly had her hand on the doorknob, looking as primed to take off and escape from him as the kid had been. He cleared his throat. "Look, I can see you're uncomfortable with me. I don't know what to say, how to make that right. But you and I never had a problem communicating before—"

"And we don't now. There's no reason business should be different than usual tomorrow."

"Business," he echoed. "There wasn't business on your mind earlier this afternoon. Or on mine. Believe me, I understand that it was Virginie's visit that changed that…and it's not like I'm blaming you for judging me—"

"I'm not judging you," she said swiftly. Too swiftly. He saw her swallow hard, and finally she turned to face him. She didn't give up her hold on that doorknob, but her voice turned soft. Molly soft. "I'm judging me, Flynn. You're right—we were becoming close. And that was never a good idea—not for me. Everything that happened this afternoon has underlined for me that I really don't know you."

"You're upset because of the baby, which God knows, I understand. But I don't know that Dylan is mine—"

"The baby's not the problem. At least not exactly. I hope I'd never tar anybody with a judgmental feather for making that kind of mistake. Everyone makes mistakes. And that particular one, couples have been making since the beginning of time." She hesitated. "But if a woman like that attracted you, Flynn, you and I honestly have nothing in common. We couldn't possibly value any of the same things."

"You've lost respect—"

"Yeah, I think that's fair to say." Her eyes mirrored the most uncomfortable kind of honesty. "You can be a real trial to work with, McGannon. You bellow and you're stubborn and you tend to railroad everyone in your path. But you've got a huge heart and an incredibly creative mind—I've never seen you judge anyone or fail to listen to their point of view. From the first day on the job, I admired you. Respected you. Enormously."

Mentally Flynn dismissed those minor details about his bellowing and stubbornness. Maybe it had taken Molly a couple of months to really believe his bark was worth peanuts—and that he really hated people kowtowing to him. But she hadn't been intimidated by him in a blue moon.

Respect was a different issue entirely. Flynn hadn't known she felt that "enormous respect." But he could feel the loss of it now—hear it, in her velvet-soft voice—and it hurt like a knife stab in his gut.

Instinctively he stepped toward her, wanting to reach her, touch her. He told himself the impulse wasn't sexual—and yet he knew it was. When he'd kissed her before, all the nuisance life differences between them disappeared. The connection had always been real, honest, and hotter than fire. Something about that chemistry created a strange, alien feeling of belonging—and maybe Flynn had never understood it, but he had a dread-sinking sensation that he'd never have that feeling again. Not with anyone. Not like with Molly. And if he just kissed her...

But the look in her eyes stopped him. She didn't back away from him. She didn't move at all in those seconds, yet she faced him with this sudden, soft, naked vulnerability in her eyes. It was a look that said *I'm a strong, tough cookie with a weakness. A weakness for you.* And yeah, she'd dive under—maybe—if he kissed her. But that wasn't the same as her willingness.

It wasn't the same as her wanting him.

His hand fell. Then both hands jammed into his pockets, buried out of sight as if he was trying to bury that impulse to touch her. "Molly, this whole story isn't done. There hasn't been time to talk to you—I haven't even had a chance to try and explain—"

She shook her head quickly, firmly. "You don't owe me any explanations, and I'm well aware you've just had your life turned upside down. But so has that baby. Love him, Flynn. And honestly, I need to go. I'll see you tomorrow."

She latched the door closed on her way out. No slam. Not even the sound of a click. She was just gone. Faster than the light bulb switched off, and leaving him with an odd, scratchy feeling in his throat.

Abruptly, though, Flynn heard a crash. He pivoted on a heel and hightailed into the living room. The floor lamp by his leather reading chair was lying on the ground, the shade rolling and punctured. The accident could have happened by osmosis, but somehow he suspected another culprit. As a point of fact, if the baby were hurt, he was going to have to shoot himself. And how could such a tiny kid manage to topple a sturdy five-foot lamp?

More terrifying yet was recognizing that the miniature monster was capable of getting into other kinds of dangerous trouble by now. Flynn whirled around again, his heart slamming…and then damn near suffered an instant stroke.

Molly may have been just a pinch right about his slightly unconventional house. Open stairs led to the second level. Two normal bedrooms were upstairs, but when Flynn had been puttering with renovations, he'd removed the walls on a third bedroom and converted it to an of-fice—Hawaiian lanai style—so that his desk overlooked the great room from the open balcony.

The baby was on the top step. He'd pulled himself up to a standing position holding on to one of the banister posts.

The toddler's diaper-heavy fanny was weaving as if he could topple over any second...and fall the whole length of the stairs.

Flynn bounded for the steps and up. Hell. Maybe he flew.

Dylan spotted him coming and let out a gleeful chortle. A *chortle*. Flynn was having a heart attack and a stroke simultaneously, and the kid was *happy*.

He sank on the steps with an arm extended to protect the monkey from falling. "So you like danger, do you? A little gamble? A little risk?"

The kid chortled harder. Flynn's lungs seemed starved for air. Yeah, he'd been this close to Dylan before, had carried the kid half the afternoon. But until that instant, he hadn't been totally alone with the baby. Until that mo-ment, every time he caught a glimpse of that rambunc-tiously wild red hair and the homely mug, he'd felt some-thing tear inside him and looked away.

"I'm thinking that one of us has to figure out how to go about feeding you. And then we have to set up some kind of place for you to sleep. Now why do I think that neither of those basic, simple projects is going to be easy?"

The baby chortled again as if he found this entire effort at conversation hilarious.

Flynn didn't. The kid had no fear—of him, of heights, of danger. And maybe Flynn could have continued to ignore the red hair and the homely face, but that character trait knotted his stomach in an acid fist.

His father had once been a designer, a big cheese engineer in the auto industry in Detroit. Aaron McGannon was brilliant at his job, took in a king's salary, and yet the family lived hand-to-mouth when Flynn was growing up. His dad couldn't stay away from a poker game or the horses. Gambling was a sickness with him.

His whole life, Flynn had not only feared—but known—that he'd inherited the same sickness. He'd never dealt a hand of poker, never touched a roulette wheel, but the seeds were there. He loved a gamble, loved a challenge. The more reckless the better. Fast cars, skydiving, white water rafting—he loved it all—and his financial success in business was nothing he could justifiably take credit for. He'd risked everything he had on some wild software ideas that had taken off, then risked all his loot on more…and probably would again. Maybe he'd helped support his mother and sister from the time he was a teenager, but that didn't change who he was. It didn't change what was inside him.

That was the reason he'd steered clear of women who wanted a wedding ring. It was the reason he never—never—wanted to be a father. Living alone, Flynn risked no one else but himself. Maybe compulsive gambling wasn't precisely a genetic trait that could be passed down, but he saw, had always seen, parts of his father's nature in himself…and damned if he'd do to a son what his dad had done to him.

"You're not mine, slugger," he whispered to Dylan.

The urchin pulled himself up by holding on to the banister rung again, and then with another chortle, hurled himself at Flynn.

He'd have fallen if Flynn hadn't caught him. Tumbled

straight down the stairs. The kid didn't seem to have an ounce of caution in his entire personality.

And Flynn's eyes squeezed closed as he hefted the little one. The baby smelled like…well, like a baby. Like baby powder and milk and other totally foreign things. The weight of him in Flynn's arms felt foreign, too, yet somehow his fanny fit just right on the seat of Flynn's arm, and the kid roped a pudgy arm around his neck as if it belonged there.

"No," he said firmly, as he carted the baby downstairs toward the kitchen. "I'm not getting attached to you— and you're not getting attached to me—so just get that thought right out of your head. I'm not your dad, and there's no way you belong with me. We're both just going to have to hang tough for a little while until this all gets straightened out. Does that sound like a plan? You ready to go pig out on beets and that icky turkey stuff in a jar Molly bought you?"

Molly…darn it, he didn't want to think of Molly again. God knew he had a giant immediate problem to handle—twenty-five chunky pounds of a crisis—and it wasn't as if he was in love with Molly. It wasn't as if they were lovers. It wasn't as if their relationship had developed into waters that murky deep. It was just…

She'd sounded ashamed of him.

And maybe, his entire life, Flynn had just been waiting for his ship to crash. The whole time he was growing up, he'd felt as if he was on a collision course with his own nature—and his dad's. No, he'd never deliberately gambled on a woman, but he'd gambled that Virginie had been telling him the truth about being on birth control. Excuses and circumstances only mattered so far. There were risks, gambles, that a good man didn't take.

But he had.

He was responsible.

Problems loomed in his mind like an endless black abyss. He didn't have a clue what he was going to do with the baby in his arms. Or how he could possibly win back Molly's respect. Hell, his self-respect had vanished like smoke since this afternoon, and he didn't even have a plan for earning that back.

There was only one thing absolutely clear to Flynn. He couldn't possibly parent a child. No one could be less qualified as a father.

The kid smacked him in the nose again. Flynn reached up to grab the little one's fist. ''Yeah, I'd be ticked if I got stuck in this situation, too. But I'll get you out of this mess, squirt, and I'll see that you're okay no matter what else happens. There's nothing for you to worry about, you hear me? Except for dinner. You up for trying some of Molly's beets?''

Four

When Molly's phone rang just after eleven, she dropped the romance novel she was reading and nearly knocked over the bedside lamp in her hustle to reach the receiver. No one called her this late. Her sometime-date Sam always called early in the evening. And she talked with her parents and sisters all the time, but no family would call at this hour unless it were really an emergency....

Apparently it was an emergency of a kind. She'd barely clapped the receiver to her ear before the baritone at the other end started talking. She almost didn't recognize Flynn. Heaven knew, his voice was distinctive, but the tone communicated such frantic anxiety that it sounded as if he was hyperventilating.

"I realize I'm the last person you probably want to hear from, and I swear I wouldn't bother you if I could help it, but dammit, Molly, I'm *desperate*—"

Molly sank back against the pillows. All evening she'd

been trying to obliterate pictures of Flynn and the baby from her mind. Nothing down that emotional road but questions she couldn't answer and insomnia and worrying she'd been trying to talk herself out of. She wanted to hear from him again tonight like she wanted a case of hives, but damn McGannon. He *did* sound desperate. "Okay, okay, take it easy, what's wro—?"

"He's crying. I had him all settled down, sound asleep, and suddenly he wakes up. Just like that. Bawling his eyes out. No reason. What the hell am I supposed to do?"

"Flynn. I'm not there. I can't possibly guess what's wrong, and I told you I didn't have any experience with babies—"

"You *have* to know something. You're a woman. You *have* to know more than me. Just give me something to do and I'll do it!"

Any other time she'd have been inclined to give him a whack upside the head for that sexist reasoning—but right then, he was obviously honestly upset. "Okay. Just calm down. And yeah, I can hear him crying in the background now...I don't see how he could possibly be sick. I mean, he had enough energy to exhaust two adults this afternoon, plenty of pep and zoom. But he's just a baby. Waking up in a strange place, his mama not there. He's probably scared, don't you think? At least start out by just trying to comfort him."

"Comfort him?"

"Yeah, you know. Like rocking him. Or carry him around for a while, patting him on the back, singing to him, stuff like that..."

"Okay, okay. I got you. Rock. Pat. Sing—"

Molly heard a sudden cracking sound so loud she winced. "Flynn? Are you still there?"

Silence. Absently she rubbed the back of her neck. In

the background she could still hear the baby crying…and then not. Apparently Flynn had dropped the phone and hustled to pick Dylan up, but had forgotten to hang up the receiver…hell's bells, knowing McGannon, he might have even forgotten he was still talking to her.

She called his name one more time…but then she heard a baritone coming from a muffled distance, singing a vaguely familiar disgusting college drinking song. Low. And badly off-key.

She hung up, not sure whether she wanted to laugh—or strangle him. For positive there wasn't a prayer of her sleeping after that, so she swung her legs out of bed.

A cup of tea might settle her down. Padding into the kitchen, she foraged in the cupboard for peppermint tea bags. She nuked a cup and sipped it as she paced around the place, thinking about men.

Outside, the only sound was the backyard maple tree, wildly tossing its branches in a fretful midnight wind. Inside, it was quieter than a tomb. She rented the upstairs of an older redbrick house belonging to the McNutts, a retired couple who spent half the year in Arizona. Their main reason for renting was fear of leaving their house deserted, but they'd had specific requirements in a tenant. No late-night noise. No parties. No *men* overnight. They told Molly she was "just ideal, dear."

Molly gulped down tea, knowing damn well she was ideal. Her parents hadn't worried when she took the job at McGannon's and moved to Kalamazoo from Traverse City. She was twenty-nine. Way old enough to be on her own and have long proven her good judgment. They knew there'd be no late nights, no parties, no *men* over, either. She'd had a reputation for being sensibly responsible, Molly mused irritably, from about the time she was four.

She straightened a picture in the living room, lined up

a book in the bookshelf that was already meticulously arranged by author and genre, gulped more tea. The refrigerator roared on. The fridge was older than she was, and the stove close to prehistoric, but she'd painted the walls pale lemon and was slowly but surely making the place her own. The couch was cream—a disastrous mistake, it showed dirt if you breathed on it, but she loved the thing, loved the cream and yellow and green Oriental rug in front of it. Her Aunt Jean's gold tea set was on the glass coffee table, her grandmother's dangling crystal lamp on the mantel, next to her one Royal Doulton figurine.

The place was neat. No dust, no messes. Every soup can was lined faceup in the cupboards, her clothes arranged in the closet by color and type. Molly could easily imagine Flynn walking into the place and first, cracking up, and then teasing her about her neatnik ways. Mercilessly.

She tried to sip more tea, discovered the cup was empty, and scowled. All the other men who'd wandered into her life would have liked her place just fine. And there'd been lots of men. Tons.

She'd dated Steve for three years in high school—and they'd stayed friends, even after he went off to the seminary. In college there'd been John, studying to be a CPA like she was. After college there'd been another John, a computer analyst. All of them had been good guys. Seriously, true-blue, downright fine responsible guys with integrity.

Damn near saints.

Impatiently Molly rinsed out her cup, popped it into the dishwasher and stalked back to bed. Not once, not once in her entire history of men, had she picked a problem. Her judgment of people was sound. She'd met her sometime-date Sam Morrison at the bank early when she moved to Kalamazoo. He was another winner. Nobody who'd give a woman a hard time at the end of an evening. Nobody she couldn't trust. Nobody who'd squeeze the toothpaste from the top or leave messy towels lying around.

Sometimes Molly thought that if she dated just one more saint, she'd die. Just up and die, collapse in a Victorian faint, from heart failure caused from boredom.

In her bedroom, she flicked off the light, punched her pillow just so and meticulously folded the sheet edge to fit precisely over the blanket. She closed her eyes, thinking, *Damn you, Molly, you're boring yourself just trying to go to sleep. What's wrong with you that you can't fall for just one of those nice guys?*

She was still awake at two-thirty in the morning—when the telephone rang again. She told herself she should be panic-stricken at a call that late, but she knew. Not just because of the call earlier, but because it was one of those women's Murphy's Laws. When you think about trouble, trouble always showed up.

She didn't even have to hear Flynn's voice before her heart started beating wicked, irresponsible drumbeats. And just a teensy bit, sympathy. He sounded as exhausted as if he'd been digging trenches in the jungle for two weeks straight.

"God, I'm sorry. I'm dead, dead, dead sorry. I wouldn't blame you for murdering me, honest I'd understand, but Molly, I—"

"I can hear him."

"Of course you can hear him. He's crying loud enough to wake the neighbors—and I don't have any neighbors for a half mile. I did the whole comforting thing—"

"Okay, okay, try and calm down—"

"Calm down? Can you hear him? I think he's sick. I think he's dying. I don't know where the nearest children's hospital is, but I can't just trust a plain old emergency room to—"

"McGannon, slow down. Maybe he *is* sick. But I think it'd make a little more sense to think about other possibilities before dragging him out in the cold in the middle of the night. You think he could be hungry?"

"There's no *way* the kid could be hungry. Hell, he ate more than me at dinner. Except for the beets. Those, he threw all over the kitchen wall. That's the *last* time I'm giving him beets, Mol—"

"Well, how about a bottle?"

"A bottle. Oh. Yeah. I remember there were some bottles in all those bags. I never got all that junk unpacked yet...."

"Well, I don't know that a baby that age even still drinks from a bottle. But maybe a little warm milk would soothe him down. And did you check his diaper?"

"I put a diaper on him before he went to bed. Actually I put on four. I don't know who the hell engineered those things, but they've got these strange tabs that it practically takes a PhD to figure out—"

"McGannon," Molly interrupted patiently, "see if he's wet."

The phone dropped—just like before. Silence followed—just like before. Molly stared at the dust motes on her ceiling, debating how many minutes to wait before hanging up, when the devil came back on the line.

"Holy kamoly."

She couldn't help but grin in the darkness. "I take it he's wet?"

"He's, um, more than wet. Geezle beezle. Hell, I'd be

screaming, too, if I were sitting in that. And the place is going to take a fumigator before this is over. Never mind that...you've got my undying gratitude for figuring it out. I love you, Mol. And I swear I'll never ask you for help again as long as I live."

The receiver clunked in her ear...not too differently than that "I love you, Mol" clunked in her heart.

She snuggled under the blankets and closed her eyes. McGannon was no saint, but she'd changed so much since knowing him. His spirit and humor and gutsy exuberance for life were all catching. He'd opened her world...which was possibly why she'd found it so impossible not to fall in love with him.

But words of love meant nothing more than lip service to Flynn—just a way of exuberantly expressing an emotion of the moment. No question the baby had totally turned his world upside down, but Molly warned herself to be cautious.

That baby could win anyone's heart. But she was no longer sure of Flynn's heart—and painfully aware that she'd talked herself into believing she knew him well. Molly Weston was infamous for being careful. She needed to fall out of love, not in deeper...which meant taking care to keep a respectable, responsible distance from Flynn McGannon.

Molly poured her third mug of sludge-strong coffee. Mornings were never her favorite time of day, but this particular morning she was prepared to snarl at anyone who looked at her crossways. Preferably McGannon— since he was responsible for her pacing the floor half the night, worrying how he was coping with the baby. She needed her eight hours sleep to be civil. She'd had three.

With a headache pounding her temples, she carried her

mug and sheath of files into Brainstorming Central. The rest of the natives were already assembled. Employees in other companies probably dreaded the Required Weekly Staff Meeting. McGannon always ran his like such a wild free-for-all that nobody missed them. Even Bailey looked perky.

Molly splashed down her coffee mug and started lining up her files. "I see Flynn's not here—anyone try rousing him from his office?"

"He's not in his office. Hasn't come in yet. Obviously I shouldn't have had a work-at-home day yesterday. I missed out on the whole story of this mystery baby." Darren looked somewhat like a funeral director in training, but his dire black attire had nothing in common with his personality. He could outgossip a Washington reporter. "I hear the woman was quite a looker."

Molly was in no mood to play Q&A—or to think about Virginie being "a looker." "Neither the lady nor the baby are any of our business. And it's not like nine o'clock is a sacred start-up time. I was just surprised he wasn't here."

Surprised was an understatement. Immediately Molly's mind traveled down dark roads of worry, imagining catastrophes that could have happened to him—or Dylan. The thing was, Flynn was one of those horrible morning people. He was no workaholic, but his favorite concentration time was five a.m. He was always in the office before everyone else. Obviously the baby had kept him up late and had upturned his normal schedule besides, but it was still totally unlike him not to call if he weren't going to be here.

Technically they could start the staff meeting without him. Flynn repeatedly claimed he was no leader, nor had any interest in that role. The purpose of the meeting was to talk about the status of their current projects, vent problems and ask for feedback and ideas, that sort of thing. With tax season coming, Molly had a few things to bring up to the crew about record-keeping, and she kept her thumb on projects going over budget. She could yell at them all without Flynn present. And they could have their idea fest without Flynn there, too…but it wasn't the same.

The damn man was a leader, whether he claimed an allergy to the role or not. He was the only one who could get Bailey to open his mouth. The only one who could soothe Simone, or get Darren off a conversational side road and back on track, or get Ralph to communicate with the older adults on their level. For damn sure, Flynn was the only one who could mediate one of the frequent wild fights that broke out when they were brainstorming—even though he claimed to love fights and preferred to be thought of as the instigator.

Maybe the baby was sick. Maybe she'd given him terrible, inadequate advice the night before and Dylan had really been ill all along. Or maybe Flynn had taken sick. The more thoughts swirled in her head, the more Molly started to panic. He was just so obviously helpless on the subject of babies. For big, boisterous Flynn to be so helpless had aroused her sense of humor the day before…darn it, some of the things he'd said and done *had* been funny. But she hadn't meant to cold-bloodedly desert either that darling baby *or* Flynn. She'd just assumed he was a smart man and he'd obviously find ways to cope. But God, what if he couldn't cope? What if…?

All of them heard the *whoosh* of the front door opening.

Molly was half rising from her chair to go call his house when she abruptly sank back down.

Flynn hurled into the office, carrying Dylan and somewhere near thirty pounds of baby paraphernalia. The baby looked adorable, wearing a football uniform with a quarterback number, his red hair slicked down with water in a grown man's hairstyle, his face shining clean.

Flynn, by contrast, looked like a refuge from a disaster. The circles under his eyes were bigger than boats. Doubtful his hair had seen a brush since yesterday, and positively he hadn't shaved. Clean navy shirt, but the shirt was as wrinkled as his khakis. One brown sock, one blue.

He bounded in, dropped the diaper bag, another bag with baby food and toys, and then parked Dylan in one of the huge easy chairs at the table as if he was just one of the guys.

"Everybody ready to work?" he asked cheerfully.

"Yeah, patent rights are complicated in this kind of situation, Ralph, but like I explained before…"

Flynn suddenly ducked his head under the table. His instincts were getting better at this. The last time the baby had been quiet for a second and a half, Dylan had managed to tip over a wastebasket and find somebody's old gum. The wastebasket now sat on top of the conference table, and the gum problem…well, the kid's hair was a little shorter on one side now. But Flynn now understood that silence and Dylan were a dangerous combination, and one flash-fast glance under the table revealed the new problem. Somehow the kid had gotten ahold of a pencil.

The baby caught sight of Flynn peering at him under the table and giggled. Then…after eighteen solid hours of parenting experience now, Flynn could have guessed this…the pencil aimed straight for his mouth.

"Now on the software application for the Gregory account—just give it to Flynn, okay, Dylan?—we really need to speed it up. Darren and Simone, I'd like you two to pair up on that... Give it to Flynn, Dylan. See? I'll give you the truck. I'll trade you for that old, dumb pencil...."

Abruptly Flynn raised his head. "Ralph, did I answer your question about that patent?"

"Yeah, basically, but I still don't quite get—"

He thought he had the pencil captured...until the urchin yanked it back—and rolled out of reach. Flynn had discovered the night before that expressing any frustration only ticked the kid off. No sane person who had experienced Dylan being ticked off would repeat the same behavior. He lowered his voice to a sweeter-than-melted-sugar tone. "Dylan, if I have to crawl under that table, you're gonna be one unhappy baby. Because if I have to crawl under that table, I'm gonna be one unhappy adult. That's it, that's it, that's a good boy, hand it here...*dammit*."

Flynn thwacked his head on the table coming back up, but he emerged, with a squalling baby under one arm and the pencil in his other hand. The smile on his face was a two-hundred-watter. "Now where were we? Darren, you talked with Guy Robinson?"

"Yeah, and I passed the project on to Bailey." Darren raised his voice to compete with the redhead. "To be honest, I don't think it can be done, but Bailey's judgment on this is better than mine."

"I don't want to have to work with Robinson," Bailey said irritably.

"You don't have to work with anyone," Flynn assured him. "But if you think this is a go, you'll need to get some cost projections in to Molly—" He caught Molly's eye. For the first time all morning. Then felt a spreading dampness under his hand.

"Um, I'll just be a second here. Ralph, did I answer

your question about patents? And we need to cover the Gregory account—''

Sweat beaded on Flynn's forehead. Was he repeating himself? And, dammit, how had the diaper bag ended up on the other side of the room?

He didn't particularly care if his staff realized he was losing his mind. Creative types never seemed to think sanity was particularly important. Neither did Flynn, but Molly's opinion was a different kettle of fish.

He whisked across the room, grabbed some diapers, whisked back to the baby. He said something to Ralph about patents, and Ralph nodded, so hopefully something intelligent had come out of his mouth. Dylan saw the diapers coming and bellowed a *"No!"* As far as Flynn could tell, it was the only word in the tyke's vocabulary, and the baby not only used it liberally but when he was deliberately trying to terrorize a grown man.

As Flynn reached for the snaps on the baby's pants, he flashed a calm, amused, confident smile, specifically at Molly. *I'm not terrorized, see? So what's a little complication of a baby in a staff meeting? I can handle this.*

He *had* to handle this. It was a matter of pride and shame. It was a matter of guilt. It was a matter of—unlike the night before—showing Molly that when a Man had a problem, a Man stepped up to the responsibility plate. He didn't duck. He didn't make excuses. He did the right thing.

A small bare foot kicked him in the chin…but he still got the sopping diaper free from the squirming urchin. Dylan had revved up the volume to a screaming pitch. Flynn didn't have a clue why he hated having his diaper changed so much. It'd help a whole lot if the baby would just stay *still* for two seconds. Maybe he was supposed to make the baby stay still, but he was too damn big and the baby too damn little and Flynn was petrified of hurting him.

"Now back to the issue of the Gregory account…" He fumbled with the tabs on the diaper, and flashed Molly another brilliant smile. *See how great I'm handling this?*

Truthfully all he'd caught were stolen miniglances at Molly so far. Long enough to see she was wearing a yellow wool blazer over a dark green skirt today. The blazer was an amazingly wild color for her, and the short skirt showed off her long, slim legs, but that ended it for the good news.

She wore the pale cream blouse buttoned strangling-tight to her throat, and although she'd met his eyes a couple of times, there was nothing there. Her eyes were as cool as a spring breeze, her facial expression locked on neutral. She hadn't looked at him with that impenetrably polite reserve from the first day—when he'd later understood she was scared of him, inside and out. By now in a staff meeting, she should be laughing; she should be frowning; she should be reaming the whole staff out about something or other to do with record-keeping. Molly *did* have an *eensy* bossy streak, and since she was the only one who could add two and two—reliably—Flynn had given her carte blanche to fix all that financial stuff. The return to a formal duchess expression told him precisely how far he'd fallen on her opinion scale.

"Flynn," Molly murmured.

His whole face brightened. She'd spoken to him; maybe they were making headway. "What, Mol? You have an accounting agenda you want to bring up?"

"I do, but possibly not quite yet. I believe you have a little problem, McGannon."

He glanced around the table. Everyone was leaned forward, elbows on the table, chins cupped in their hands...which was a little curious, considering that everybody usually lounged through these staff meetings in fully relaxed fashion. And then Molly motioned with a finger, pointing down.

He looked down. There was a diaper in his hands. And the bottom half of a pair of football toddler pajamas lying on the floor. But no baby.

The little one was crawling, streaking the whole staff with his bare fanny, and headed for the open door at the speed of sound.

went around the table, chairs crammed too close together, which was a little crazy, considering there's nobody home... the real thing is they all... together in jolly rooked silence. And then Molly removed Saint Ben... smiling down...

...rocked again, there was a flicker in his baby-soft skin hip of...

The little guy was crawling again by the wrong road with his face fiercely, and headed for the open door at the speed of a hare.

Five

Flynn wasn't sure how it happened. He'd set up a low-slung white hammock a few days before so Dylan would have a place to nap. He'd deliberately located the hammock right next to his desk. The kid hated sleeping, let everyone know at decibel volume that he was violently opposed to naps and bedtimes, but the baby seemed to think it was cool that he could climb into the hammock on his own. And when Dylan finally dropped off, Flynn had a slim prayer of getting some work done if he just reached over and rocked the hammock from time to time.

And that's how it was. One minute Dylan was snoozing. Flynn had one hand extended to keep the hammock rocking, and the other was tap-dancing his computer keys. Blinds were half-drawn to dilute the bright October sunshine pouring in.

The next minute—as if a magician had suddenly waved a magic wand—Molly was sitting in the chair next to his desk. Her chin was propped under a curled-up fist, as if she'd been sitting there studying him for a while. She was doing the duchess routine with clothes today—lace at the collar and throat, cameo earrings, a tediously long camel skirt. Nothing unusual about Molly being properly dressed for a D.A.R. tea, but the expression on her face was.

She hadn't unstiffened around him in days. At that moment, though, her face was luminous with emotion—a frown pleating her forehead, her soft eyes radiating worry. "Are you okay?" she asked quietly.

"Sure, I'm okay." He couldn't imagine where the question came from.

"When I walked in here, I found you sound asleep, sitting up. And I didn't mean to wake you—I just wasn't sure what to do. You look seriously exhausted, Flynn."

"No, no, I wasn't asleep. I couldn't have been asleep. I was just concentrating hard on a project…" Well, he had been. But a screen saver showed up on his computer monitor instead of the figures he'd been working on. And somehow the bright October sunshine had suddenly turned into a gloomy, drizzly rain that was driveling down the windows. Disoriented, Flynn glanced at the baby—Dylan hadn't budged—and then his watch. How could it possibly be three o'clock?

"The baby's keeping you up nights, isn't he? You've come in looking more worn-out every morning. I'm afraid you're going to get sick if you don't stop trying to burn the candle at both ends—"

"I'm not worn-out and I'm as healthy as a horse." Flynn dry-washed a hand over his face, aware he sounded cranky. The last thing he wanted to do was bark at Molly, but his mood was as groggy as a crab's. He needed a minute to recover from the nap he sure as hell hadn't been having. "I'm guessing you popped in here for a reason?"

"Yes, of course I did. I've got some papers for you to sign." Yet Molly hesitated, studying him for another trudging long moment. Sheesh. Flynn could remember when she jumped if he barked. These days he wasn't positive a tornado would intimidate her. Thankfully, though, she seemed to make up her mind to drop the personal subjects. Nothing ever diverted Molly as fast as work.

Efficiently she shuffled some forms in front of him, uncorked the lid on a pen and gave him that, too. He was being as good as gold, angling the pen to sign up a storm—but that didn't please her, either.

"McGannon! *Look* at what you're signing!"

"Why?"

"Because. How many times do I have to give you this lecture? For all you know, I'm absconding with the company funds, giving away the bank, setting you up for a fraud problem with the IRS. There are certain financial things you shouldn't trust anyone with."

Her voice was barely a whisper—both of them had automatically lowered their voices to avoid waking the baby—but she was still metaphorically yelling at him. Molly had been painfully polite with him for days. He scribbled his John Henry on all her forms with a grin. "Yeah, I heard parts of that lecture before, Ms. Weston. It's good advice. I even follow it with ninety-nine percent of the people I know. But I'd bet my last dollar that anything you give me is straight to the penny."

"You're hopeless." Molly took the papers back with a sigh, then glanced at the baby. "He looks as snug as a bug in a rug. Dylan really loves that hammock, doesn't he?" she murmured.

"Yeah, he does. Just don't tell him it's a *b-e-d*, okay? Don't use the *s-l-e-e-p* word, either." Flynn had hung the hammock low, not just so the baby could climb in on his own, but so falling out couldn't hurt him. There was nothing beneath him but a thick blanket over plush-thick carpet. "He almost always falls asleep the minute he piles in there and curls up. You try saying the word 'nap' to the kid, though, and the temper tantrum isn't worth your life."

"I've heard. We've all heard," Molly said wryly. "You realize we've all fallen in love with him."

He realized that the staff—at least temporarily—seemed reasonably charmed by having a baby around. Even Bailey. But it was Molly's eyes that turned tender around the little one, Molly who talked to Dylan and scooped him up for a snuggle—even when she was obviously trying to keep a distance. She sure had no trouble keeping a distance from *him* for the past few days, though. Until now.

He'd signed all her papers, yet now she crossed her legs as if she intended staying awhile. "You're in trouble with him, Flynn," she said gently.

"You think I don't know that? The kid's barely a year old, and already you can't tell him anything. In every confrontation so far, the score card ends up the same. Dylan—ace. McGannon—zero."

Molly chuckled, but the dancing humor in her eyes didn't last long. "I think you're in over your head," she said quietly. "You look exhausted. Seriously exhausted. You're trying to run the business as if nothing had changed, and care for the baby full-time. No one could do that, Flynn. Something has to give."

"I'm doing fine," he assured her swiftly. Possibly that was a lie of epic proportions, but he'd been stone-flat determined not to ask for Molly's help again. He wasn't exactly sure what he needed to prove to her, but he wanted her regard back. Hell, he wanted Molly back. The way they'd been together before.

"Couldn't you shift some work around? Let Simone take up some slack? Or Darren?"

"I've already considered that. Those two are the closest to understanding my specific projects. And down the pike, there are a number of things I could rearrange about the business. But not overnight. And not when I honestly don't know *what* to plan or prepare for." Flynn sighed, stretching out his long legs. "Frankly every time the phone rings I jump, thinking it has to be Virginie."

"I take it she hasn't called yet?"

Flynn shook his head. "I still can't believe she hasn't shown up to take Dylan back." He paused. He wasn't sure what had brought this conversation on, but since Molly hadn't asked before, he hadn't filled her in. Now she seemed settled in to listen, but he wasn't sure what was right to tell her. "I talked to my lawyer. And my doc."

"And what'd you find out?"

Flynn dragged a hand through his hair. "Used to be, it took a blood test from the dad and the baby to test for DNA, but there are newer, better tests now. All they do is take a swab from the cheek cells inside the mouth. It won't hurt him, no needles. So we're both having that done on Monday."

"And that'll prove for sure if you're the father?"

"Nothing's for sure. But I was told these newer tests are 99.9 percent accurate. Some labs can take a month to get back, but the actual test doesn't take a week's time. My doc said he'd push to get the results as pronto as possible. The problem is…aw, hell, Molly. Yeah, I'm getting that test done. Obviously I have to know the paternity issue for sure. But originally I thought those results were the whole cheese—everything'd be solved if I knew that answer?—only nothing's turning out that simple. Every question I asked my lawyer only raised more questions and problems.''

"Like what?"

"Like custody issues are complicated." Flynn lurched out of his chair, wide-awake now and way too frustrated to sit still. "Legally there's no immediate sweat right now about the baby being with me. My name's listed as the dad on the birth certificate. Whether that's true or not true—if I start raising legal questions about that, some things get put in motion that I'd have no power over."

Molly, frowning, pushed out of her chair, too. They both instinctively aimed for the farthest corner of the room, where there was the least chance of Dylan hearing them and waking up. "Such as?"

"Such as…Social Services could take the kid away." Flynn had been bottling up the worry for days. He couldn't help it spilling out. "Jake—my lawyer—said Virginie's deserting the baby would raise questions about her being a fit mother. I can't say I'm not worried about that myself. She sure didn't seem stable the day she flew in here. But if I contend the kid isn't my responsibility, either, Social Services would likely put him in foster care until the whole thing was resolved."

Molly cocked her head. "So you don't *have* to take responsibility for the baby until or unless your paternity is proven? For heaven's sakes, McGannon, I could have sworn that was what you wanted?"

"*Mol.*" Sheesh. Flynn couldn't remember her ever being this obtuse before. "I'm *not* putting a thirteen-month-old baby in foster care. With strangers. With no say over who they are, or if they'll give a damn about him or take good care of him or anything else. That's completely out of the question.''

"Ah," she murmured.

"What the Sam Hill is that *ah* supposed to mean?"

"He's growing on you," she said.

"He is *not* growing on me. This is a matter of his being a pipsqueak-size hellion. A one-year-old bad-tempered curmudgeon of a hellion. But temporarily he seems to be *my* hellion, and whatever happens to him after this, it has to be right. For him. So I know he'll be okay."

"Uh-huh."

"Quit smiling at me, Weston. You're starting to tick me off. I'm telling you this turns into a worse mess every time I turn around. I tried calling some pediatricians. There's about ten million of them in town, so you'd think that'd be easy, wouldn't you?"

"I take it you ran into more complications."

"I couldn't believe it. I just want the kid checked out, you know, his own doc in case he got sick. Obviously I can't wait for an emergency to line that up. So I started calling these offices, and I got all this grief—two of those receptionists actually hung up on me."

"I'll be darned," Molly said dryly. "Not that I've known you for a while, but on a wild guess did you make them feel intimidated by grilling them half to death?"

"Hey. I have every right to ask about a doc's credentials before trusting a kid's life in their hands. And I finally found one. Marginally a maybe. Dr. Owen Milbrook. Harvard Medical School, pediatric internship in Boston. Appointment at four tomorrow. Of course just because he has some reasonably acceptable credentials doesn't mean he isn't a jerk. If Dylan doesn't like him, I'm hauling the kid right out of there."

"Flynn?"

"What?"

"I promised myself I wouldn't do this," Molly murmured, "but I swear you could tempt a saint. C'mere, you."

Flynn didn't have a clue what she meant, but when she suddenly grabbed his shirt, he assumed she wanted him to lean down closer. They'd both been whispering, both huddled in the far corner of the room for the same reason—neither wanted to wake the baby. And his head was already bent, hers raised, so they could hear each other better. It seemed a logical bet that she felt frustrated trying to communicate anything clearly at that whisper-volume.

Like his gambling father, Flynn should have known better than to bet.

He suspicioned his judgment was mistaken when her lips slammed on his. He picked up another telltale clue when her fingers loosened their hold on his shirt and her arms lassoed his neck.

It was a hell of a mystery—what the Sam Hill motivated the sudden reward of a kiss from Molly, when the last he knew, she was ashamed of him. But Flynn's interest in the mystery fizzed out in about a second and a half. Maybe faster.

He tuned out the office. Tuned out the sound of drumming rain and a distant phone ringing. Tuned out the baby.

He tuned in to Molly. Life had an amazing way of decomplicating when Molly was in his arms. If possibly she only intended a fast smack, he wasn't going to waste the moment by analyzing. He kissed her back.

Nothing complicated about that.

Since her arms were already looped around his neck, his were free to roam, sliding against her silk blouse, shaping down her shoulders and spine. Her scent, her textures, went straight to his head like a double shot of scotch. Her body lay flush against his, her breasts warm and tight, coiling his hormones to trigger awareness. Nothing complicated about any of that, either.

She tasted like his worst nightmare. Always had. As a kid, he had a recurring dream where he was running, running, chasing something he understood was critical to his survival, only he'd wake up, always without it, always without knowing what it was. That was her. Her mouth was smaller than his, her lips softer, more supple, sweeter…but it wasn't that. He tasted longing with Molly. A longing for something he didn't understand, a nameless, luring need that made air and water and shelter seem no-account survival issues by comparison. Desire charged through his bloodstream, hot and compelling, but Flynn could isolate that as nothing more dangerous than hormones. That wicked, winsome, bluesy-sax feeling of longing…no other woman had ever invoked it. No other woman had ever provoked it.

She surfaced for air. For an instant she searched his face, her eyes veiled and smoky, as if confused how one fast slam of a kiss could possibly have inspired so much trouble.

He dipped his head for another kiss. It was the only answer he could give her. His mouth rubbed against hers, rough-soft, wooing, until her lips parted. When his tongue found hers, her fingers clenched responsively tight around his neck.

He backed up against the carpeted wall, pulling her with him, cradling her against the V of his thighs. Tongues touched and teased, in a damp dark kiss that kept diving deeper. Her blouse kindly slipped from the waistband of her skirt, and his fingers suddenly discovered skin. Warm, mobile skin that molded for his touch, heated under his palms.

She tilted her head, inhaled another lungful of air, came back. Her fingers riffled through his hair, framing his head, taking a hot openmouthed kiss like a freight train had better not try getting in her way. Heat pulsed through him like fire, licking through his veins, smoking fresh sparks wherever she touched. Sexual heat, he told himself. Not need. A dangerous thought, that he could need anyone this much, and right then thinking was the last thing he wanted to do. A man could drown in the rich, wild emotion pouring out of Molly. If there was a life buoy in those deep waters, Flynn had no interest in finding it.

His palms slid down to her fanny, cupping her intimately closer, until his arousal pressed against her abdomen. He rubbed. She rubbed back. He heard the whisper-slide of stockings when she tried to wind a leg around his. He pushed again at the confounded silky blouse fabric in his way, found the double hook of her bra. He couldn't see it, didn't need to see to know it was snow white and utilitarian, a puritan bra because that's who Molly was.

But not then. He'd known forever that her buttoned-down primness was only the public Molly, known there was a warm giver of a woman beneath that layer. But not like this.

Whatever unleashed the tigress in Molly, he had no time to analyze. All he knew was that he'd been pit-low for days, about himself and his life, and somehow he was someone else with her. Molly could make a man believe he was worth gold even when he knew better. He stroked the swell of her breast, the caress meant to be cherishing, tender. The nub tip was swollen, as vulnerable as she was, her responsiveness spearing desire through him with stunning power.

She arched against his hand with a groan, a velvet-soft sound of frustration...or maybe he was the one making

that frustrated, urgent sound. He whispered kisses down
her jaw to her throat—but her throat was exasperatingly
covered by a high-necked collar with a bunch of frothy
lace. He tried to more fully explore those exquisitely sensitive breasts of Molly's, but straps and fabric tangled in
his way.

She had a thousand too many clothes sabotaging any
real freedom to touch, and heat was spiraling between
them faster than a volcano. He wanted her prone, not upright. He wanted her naked on a hard mattress, not pressed
up against a scratchy carpeted wall in an office. His eyes
shuttered open on the rainy windows, the baby in the hammock…and suddenly everything was wrong.

"Mol…" She didn't seem real inclined to surface. Hell,
neither was he. He tried trailing softer, soothing kisses
down her cheek, her temple, instead of that volcanic kind.
He tried removing his hand from temptation and smoothing her blouse back down to cover her up. He tried to
impale the word 'no' in his head, but his mind was on an
entirely different kind of impaling.

"Hey, tiger, look at me. Just for a second, okay?" Finally she raised her head, but hell. Those sleepy eyes and
red, soft, tremulous mouth almost took him under all over
again. "Mol…"

He couldn't explain the alarm bells suddenly going off
in his head. It was just…they'd never traveled down this
road so far before. And it suddenly mattered. What inspired that sudden impulsive kiss from Molly. What unleashed that unforgettably sensual tigress. God knew
Flynn hated to look a gift horse in the mouth…but from
the minute the baby entered the picture, Molly really
hadn't seemed all that fond of Flynn McGannon.

He pushed a strand of hair from her cheek. "In two
seconds flat, love, I could have the door closed and locked

and protection dug up from somewhere. But I need to be sure that's what you want, that you wouldn't regret it.''

"I..." She stiffened so quickly, stepped back from his arms so fast—and her balance was so rocky—that he reached out to hold her steady.

Then dropped his hands. He could see it in her eyes. The magic fading, reality slamming in. She pushed at her tumbled hair with shaky fingers. "I can't believe either of us let this go so far. We're in the middle of your office. And the baby's right here—"

"The baby's still sound asleep. No one saw anything, no one heard anything. The only thing that happened was between you and me." And Flynn was afraid he'd never get it back. That intimate connection. For a few minutes, he'd been her love. A man with the right to know her, take her, claim the magic of Molly Weston—and that incredible responsiveness of hers was still kindling flash fires in his pulse. But she sure wasn't looking at him the same way now.

"I'm sorry, Flynn. Sincerely sorry." She was suddenly terribly busy, straightening, tucking, smoothing. In front of his eyes she was metamorphosing from passionate, abandoned lover back into prim, proper Molly. "I *know* I started this by kissing you first, but I honestly never meant anything like this to happen—"

"So help me understand why that happened. Why *did* you kiss me?" He snagged her wrist, just for a moment—before she'd metamorphosed so completely that any chance of wooing any honest answer from her was gone. "The chemistry was no surprise—there's been combustible chemistry between us from the first. Until the baby entered the picture. And that's just it, Mol—you've barely talked to me in days. So the last thing I was expecting was your suddenly volunteering a kiss."

"Well, I didn't plan it, either." As soon as her hand was free, she tucked her arms protectively under her chest. Her face was flushed, her voice fumbling. "It was just when you started talking about the baby...darn it, Flynn, maybe you don't see it, but you're adorable around Dylan. Even more so because you're so obviously scared of him. I never expected to see you scared of anything. And more than that...watching you these past few days, I can see how over your head you are, how totally your world's been turned upside down...."

She felt sorry for him. And maybe Flynn's hormones needed a dunk in ice water, but that didn't make him feel better. Humor and sympathy were the last things in the universe he wanted to arouse in Molly. Her believing he was scared of the baby was even worse.

He *was* scared of the pipsqueak. But how the Sam Hill had she guessed? Cripes, since this whole thing started, he'd been trying to handle the problem of Dylan alone, no ducking the responsibility, no whining, no showing anyone—and especially not Molly—that he was petrified.

"Now, McGannon, I can see from the expression on your face that I must have offended you." Molly hustled over to scoop up the papers on his desk and then edged for the door. "I never meant to sound critical. The exact opposite is true. In fact, that's why I first walked in here...yeah, I had some forms for you to sign...but I also wanted to apologize. I was afraid I'd come across before as judgmental, and I wanted to offer some help."

"Help?"

She nodded. "It's a pretty worthless offer—I told you before I don't know anything about babies. But you've been coming in looking more exhausted every day. I'm afraid you'll get sick if you don't get some rest—"

"I'm fine," he said impatiently, and then hesitated.

"Unless you think I'm doing something wrong with the kid—"

"No, nothing like that. Good grief, McGannon, anybody can see he's thriving and happy. You're the one who's getting run-down. It's not like you had time to arrange for this sudden surprise in your life...and it has to be hard to even guess what to do as far as baby-sitters, or streamlining your work, or whatever, without knowing for sure how long Dylan's going to be with you. But that's the point. Now is when you obviously need some help. For instance...do you want some company to go with you for that pediatrician's checkup?"

"I can handle it," Flynn said irritably. Although truthfully his mind had already conjured up a preview of the horror movie to come. Dylan hated anything that interfered with his mobility, which meant trying to keep him still and quiet in a doc's office rated up there as a shuddering challenge. Flynn could easily picture the baby hollering bloody murder, while he tried to juggle diaper bags and toys and attempt an intelligent conversation with the doctor....

"Quit being so damn touchy—I didn't say you couldn't handle it, Flynn. I asked if you wanted some company."

"Well, yes." And then swiftly he shook his head. "No."

"How decisive," Molly murmured dryly.

"You don't realize what you're volunteering for. I can't ask you to face Armageddon with me."

She chuckled. "Now, come on. With two adults, how hard can it be to take one small baby to a doctor?"

Molly, of course, hadn't been living day and night with Dylan the way he had.

Once she left the office, Flynn sank into his desk chair and stared at the snoozing baby. Possibly—almost inconceivably—he was looking forward to the doctor's visit because Molly was going to be with him.

The truth was, he loved being with her. And he wanted her company. But he wanted her company the way it used to be—in that yesteryear when his pride and manhood were intact and Molly enjoyed being with him and he was somebody good in her eyes. On an evolutionary time scale, that historical yesteryear could be pinned down to B.B. A week ago. Before the Baby.

The baby had changed everything—rocked his life, shaken all the values he thought were secure, stolen his sleep, threatened his sanity. Nothing was the same. Somehow, though, he'd never anticipated this particular catch-22.

The last thing he wanted was Molly kissing him—or spending time with him—out of pity. Yet he had to find ways to spend time with her if he was ever going to rewin her respect.

His behavior, of course, was the key. He had to show her that he wasn't an irresponsible, weak philandering kind of jerk but the kind of man who faced up to a problem and handled it competently, responsibly, seriously.

Hell. If he could prove that to her, maybe he could even convince himself.

Six

Molly fully anticipated the pediatrician's appointment to be a trial. She wouldn't have volunteered to go with Flynn otherwise. The baby was a heart-stealing darling, but Dylan just had a teensy tendency to be a handful. She expected some ticklish moments from the baby. Instead, it was the baby's father who was proving to be a royal pistol and a half.

Dr. Milbrook met her eyes across the room. He winked—not for the first time since this office visit started. Owen was a small, slim, dignified man with neatly brushed gray hair and a no-nonsense demeanor. His eyes, though, could twinkle like Santa's. Molly had the sneaky feeling that Owen had crossed paths with panic-stricken parents before.

She couldn't see Flynn's face—he was hovering over the examining table with his back to her. But she could see Dylan, squirming in every direction in spite of dad and doc. And likely a bystander in the waiting room could hear Flynn's booming voice.

"Exactly what are you doing now?"

"Just checking the baby's reflexes—"

"You're not going to hit him with that hammer, are you?"

"Uh-huh." Said hammer hit said reflex, resulting in a predictable bellow from Dylan. The baby quit giving the doctor grief as soon as the hammer was removed from sight, though, where Flynn kept turning more pale.

"I want you to tell me ahead if you're going to do anything that could hurt him."

"At the moment I just want to listen to his heart—which is going to be more than a little challenging if I'm trying to talk to you at the same time. I take it this is your first child, Mr. McGannon?"

"It's not that. Dylan...he just isn't like anybody else's kid."

"I realized that right away," Dr. Milbrook said gravely. "In fact, it's hard to imagine a more special, precious child than this one. But if it would reassure your mind any, I've been doing this for nineteen years. I swear I've never lost a child during a checkup yet—and almost always, the parents manage to survive it, too. I promise, it's okay for you to sit down and relax."

"You don't understand. You don't know him. He has a slight temper—"

"Trust me. I've seen children have temper tantrums before."

"And he can move faster than greased lightning—"

"In all these years, I've never dropped a baby. Even those that can move faster than greased lightning."

Flynn was mollified—for thirty seconds. Molly crossed

her legs, watching him, feeling amused and bemused and confused all at once.

Of course she'd seen Flynn's exasperating side at work. His enthusiasm and energy had always been so boundless that he tended to overpower anything in his path. He cared about people; he was just short on sensitivity. He seemed unaware that the rest of the world didn't automatically roar through life at his breakneck speeds or stereophonic volumes.

McGannon could be hopeless, but she'd never seen him as bad as he was with the baby...the baby he wasn't supposed to want. The baby he kept claiming wasn't his.

Molly fretfully tugged on an earring. Days before, she'd sworn to do the safe thing and keep a distance from Flynn and his baby problem. She'd meant to. Watching him cope with Dylan in the office, though, was like watching a gangly moose with a priceless piece of bone china. He wasn't just awkward with the tyke. He seemed to think the child would break if he breathed too hard. And every day he'd come into the office looking more gaunt-cheeked and hollow-eyed.

She found it bewildering that his family hadn't shown up. In *her* clan, the advent of a baby would have brought relatives out of the woodwork, running to help. But Flynn never mentioned his family, and no one seemed to be helping him—not with advice, not with time, not with anything. The staff had cottoned to a baby around the office with no sweat, but that group was so eccentric and so busy with their own real work that no one had really stepped in. Molly simply had to offer him some help.

That didn't, of course, explain how she'd ended up plastered all over him that afternoon. That embrace kept seeping into her mind. The deep, dark, drugging kisses. His touch like the stroke of a shiver. The lush, wild, com-

pelling feeling, emanating from him, that he needed her.
Really needed. Like loneliness was a devil fire inside him,
and holding her could make or break him.

She knew that couldn't really be true. Even allowing
the thought to surface made Molly feel impatient with
herself. Flynn was a vital, virile, magnetic package. She
just had no experience with that kind of potent sexuality.
He'd also brought her out of her shell as no one else ever
had, creating a bond that Molly had so easily, so naively,
assumed was love.

Every time she looked at the baby, that assumption bit
the dust. Men always seemed able to separate sex from
love differently than women, but Flynn obviously hadn't
loved Virginie. He barely remembered her name. And it
frightened Molly, threatened her, to realize how easily that
could have been her—someone Flynn slept with and forgot. She'd presumed his caring, presumed he had real feelings for her. And now that mistake kept slapping her
heart. She didn't know him. At all. Not in any way that
mattered.

Yet the oddest thought kept surfacing in her mind that
Flynn didn't know himself, either. Because the more she
saw him with the baby, the more she saw sides to Flynn
McGannon that seemed to bewilder him—a lot more than
her.

Dylan let out a sudden squalling bellow, and Molly
instinctively surged to her feet.

"Molly—" Flynn's head whipped around her, seeking
her as if she were a beacon in a storm.

"I'm here. And I can see you two could use a little
help. Come to Molly, big guy." The exam was done, and
the doctor was obviously trying to have a conversation
with Flynn. The baby had a slightly different game plan.
He wanted down. Now. He'd had enough of being fussed

over and he had that look in his eyes—Molly had seen it in the office—they were all going to pay in earsplitting volumes if things didn't start going his way pronto.

Dylan liked being naked a ton more than he liked being dressed...shades of his father, Molly thought with dark humor. But twenty minutes later, the baby was dressed, the bill paid and the whole doctor's-visit ordeal was over.

Molly sat in the cramped back seat of Flynn's Lotus on the drive back to the office. She still had to pick up her car. Traffic was thick at five o'clock. Cars honking, bumper-to-bumper tempers. The sky was darkening with a spit of snow in the air.

Flynn had thanked her—several times—for coming with him, but then fallen as silent as a stone. There was every reason for him to be quiet, Molly recognized. He was exhausted. Traffic was heavy. And Dylan had engaged him in a game—the baby threw a toy, then yelped his misery about being able to reach it, then Flynn picked it up—and the baby chortled as he "accidentally" dropped the toy again. Dylan was tickled pink with the game.

Molly was just as charmed.

And Flynn had his hands full between the traffic and the baby, but his silence started to gnaw on Molly. The thing was, McGannon never shut up. He was either roaring laughter or roaring temper, but a peaceful stretch of silence was totally out of character.

Finally she spoke up. "You ended up liking Dr. Milbrook better than you expected?"

"He seemed okay."

The short answer told her nothing. She leaned forward, but the car was too shadowed for her to catch his expression. "I'm guessing you felt some relief that Dylan got such a great bill of health. A sturdy, strapping boy, healthy as a horse...."

"Yeah. But you heard him. About the diaper rash."

Molly blinked. That was the reason for all this broody silence? "Flynn, the doc said it was about impossible to find a baby who'd never had a diaper rash. And that it was no big thing, you just use this cream—"

"He didn't have it when I first got him."

"So?"

"So it was my fault he got it."

Was this how it was going to be? Every time she tried to harden her heart against caring too much, he said some damn fool stupid thing that sabotaged her all over again? "McGannon, you're being a numbskull," she said humorously. "The baby is *fine*. You heard Dr. Milbrook say that every which way from Sunday—"

"He got a diaper rash, because I didn't know what I was supposed to do. How many hundreds of things could there be like that? Where I could hurt the kid because I don't know anything. He fell off a chair yesterday. Damn near killed himself. Hell, I was right there, but he climbed up on the thing and pitched over the side so fast I couldn't stop him."

"Come on. You're expecting yourself to know stuff that no first-time parent knows. How could they? Babies survive."

"Survive and thrive are two different things. Every man isn't cut out to be a father. You can do too damn much harm if you screw up." Abruptly Flynn checked the rearview mirror, pulled over to the side of the road, stopped, picked up Dylan's toy from the floor, then resumed driving. "And to be honest, I don't believe I have any instincts for this fathering business."

Molly couldn't hold back a chuckle.

"You're *laughing* at me?" Flynn snapped.

"Yeah, I am. You're adorable at this fathering business. I swear you're the only one who can't see it."

"Weston, you call me adorable one more time today and I swear I won't be responsible. Nobody has *ever* called me adorable."

"You just stopped the car to give the baby a toy," she pointed out gently.

"So what? I had to. He would have cried if I hadn't."

"Uh-huh. You're a classic study for a mean, uncaring guy all right. No instinct for fathering at all."

"Would you quit making jokes? I'm trying to have a serious conversation with you. You made it crystal clear that your opinion of me dropped to slug level when this baby showed up. You don't think a good man would have gotten himself into this kind of mess—"

"Now, I told you, I never meant to sound judgmental that way—"

"The point is—I agree with you. But if you have magic answers about what I'm supposed to do now, I sure don't. The kid deserves a future, the best life it's possible to give him. And regardless where his set of genes came from, I somehow got a vote in affecting what that could be. But I won't be less than honest about this, Mol. Whether I'm his dad or not, his best shot at a future may not be with me."

Molly hesitated, then said swiftly, "Keep going." She could see the driveway to the business looming ahead. She never liked making fast, impulsive decisions—the few times she had, they never worked out well—but this time she felt she had no choice.

Flynn seemed confused at the instant change in conversation. "Beg your pardon?"

"Don't turn in at the office. Just drive to my place. It's

only a few blocks from here—three lights up and then turn right.''

"I don't understand—"

"I know. But I've been listening to you leap to these big, gigantic conclusions about your fitness as a father—based on one extremely small diaper rash. I suppose it wouldn't be exactly p.c. to tell the boss that he's a basket case, but—''

"Mol—''

"—But it's obvious to me that you're not just cranky but too tired to think straight. I'm offering to feed you both dinner. And since this is a one-time offer, not to be repeated and nonredeemable, I'd think real hard before turning it down.''

Sympathy again. Flynn knew damn well the offer for dinner came from her feeling sorry for him. But he'd been curious about where and how she lived for a blue moon, and besides that, he was damned determined to show her he was no basket case. So he went along with the plan—that is, until she unlocked the door to her upstairs apartment and he stepped inside.

One glance at her living room made him tighten his hold on Dylan. "Holy cow. We can't come in. This just isn't going to work, Mol. Dylan and white furniture…God. No. The potential for disaster boggles the mind, and I'm not exaggerating.''

She chuckled—and closed the door. "Yeah, I thought of that. But your angel'd be doing me a favor if he wrecked that cream couch. Stupidest thing I ever bought. It looked so pretty in the store, but it's so impractical it's driving me crazy. Don't worry about it.''

She dropped the baby's diaper bag, peeled off her coat, and then waggled her fingers at Dylan. The baby immediately dare-devil-dove straight for her arms. "Boy, are you a chunk, cutie. How about if you and I figure out dinner while we let your dad relax? Flynn, this invitation was pretty impromptu. I think I have some red wine around, or some tea, but I probably can't offer you much to drink besides that."

"I don't need anything. And just tell me what you want me to do as far as helping with dinner."

But she banished him from the kitchen—after handing him a glass of red wine, apparently whether he wanted it or not. He could hear her clattering pans around and *coo-chee-cooing* to Dylan, while he was stuck all by himself with bossy instructions to put his feet up and relax.

Flynn knew better than to try relaxing, and his loneliness didn't last long. He gulped down the wine just as he saw the baby scuttling across the doorway on all fours.

He knew that look in the tyke's eyes. Nothing made Dylan happier than a Search and Destroy mission in a new place.

Flynn jammed down the wineglass and started jogging. Faster than a blink, he lifted a vase, picture frame and a gold tea set thing to her mantel...then abruptly chased across the room, pushed two table lamps out of the baby's reach, scooped up a terrifyingly fragile-looking china thingamabob and put that high. The kid, by then, had pulled himself to a standing position at the coffee table. Weaving like a Saturday night drunk, he happily babbled enthusiasm for all Flynn's running around. "Gabalob? Mabloo?"

"Yeah, you like new places, don't you?" Aw hell, he hadn't seen the magazines on the coffee table until it was too late. Dylan scrunched up a cover of *Newsweek,* and most disrespectfully, popped the picture of the president into his mouth. "No, no, didn't we talk about your eating paper before?"

The kid chortled and went down on all fours when he realized Flynn was willing to give chase. He liked experimenting with a two- or three-step walk, but his top speed was a crawl and the kid knew it.

"Whoops. Where'd my co-cook go...?" Molly flew in from the doorway.

"Um, Mol, we had a little problem with your *Newsweek.* I think the kid has already decided his political leanings, because the current president is being chewed up and spit out—"

"No sweat. Watch the news some days, and I've been tempted to do the same thing myself." Molly grinned, but he saw the look in her eyes. Damned if he could understand it. Discouragement had been stalking his mood— he'd just wanted to do something right in Molly's eyes, and somehow the pediatrician's visit had turned into a black humor comedy of every darned thing he was doing wrong. Yet for some confounded reason, her gaze rested on his face with a look softer than melted butter. "I caught that yawn, Flynn."

"I didn't yawn. And I'm not tired."

"Uh-huh. You're just ornery enough to growl at a butterfly. This time I'm taking the baby and closing the kitchen door. You sit down and put your feet up, or I'm going to have to get mean."

"Sheesh. Were you this bossy when I hired you?"

She lifted her eyebrows. "Hey, you hired an overshy introvert who used to get stomachaches if she had to raise her voice. You're the one who corrupted me, so don't waste your time complaining. The menu for dinner is extremely fancy. Mac and cheese, soup, toast, ice cream. Actually I could put something more serious together for the adults, but there was only so much I had around for the one-year-old set.''

''That's fine for me, too. Anything but beets.''

She chuckled again, scooped up the baby and reaimed for the kitchen—but not before wagging a royal finger at him. ''Sit.''

Hell, she was treating him like a dog. On the other hand, she'd barely disappeared from sight before another yawn escaped him. He dry-washed a hand over his face and plunked down on her couch...just for a minute.

Chasing after Dylan had kept him too busy to really notice much. He pushed off his shoes—petrified of getting dirt anywhere near her white couch, and the Persian rug looked just as sacred—and then leaned back, inhaling a real taste for the view this time. A study of the room started to perk up his spirits.

The cream and pale yellow colors were just like her. So was everything about the place. Clean, soft colors. Pictures hung just so. No dust, no dirt, no clutter. In the far corner, there was a six-legged antique desk that looked so spindly it would break if a guy breathed on it. The bay window had a window seat with a bunch of pillows in apricot, vanilla and lemon colors. Lacy edges. A few knickknacky kind of things that looked petrifyingly fragile.

Relief swept through him when he realized the obvious. He didn't belong here. For the first time since that confounded embrace this afternoon, Flynn felt tight muscles finally start to unknot. Somehow he'd felt a connection to Molly, a need, that still curled hot embers around his nerves.

Well, that had to be nothing more than chemistry. Hormones. Because all he had to do was glance around to know he didn't belong with Molly. She was a neatnik. He walked in with wet boots. White couches and formal antiques suited her. A basketball hoop in the office suited him.

Flynn yawned again, sinking deeper into the plump couch cushions as he mentally warmed up on this whole theme. She was prissy. Judgmental. Puritanical in her values. Hell, there was so damn much wrong with her that he had no idea why he thought about her a hundred times a day. Why should he care what Molly thought of him? Why did it make so much blasted difference that she was ashamed of him?

Well, it did, Flynn thought irritably. Because Molly brought up issues—and so did the kid—that lay on his conscience like concrete. He'd never wanted to turn out like his father. Maybe he had the same addiction to risk, but he thought he'd meticulously arranged his life so his gambling streak couldn't hurt anyone else.

Only he had. The sound of the baby's bubbling laughter behind the closed kitchen door was the most painful kind of proof. He'd never meant to risk a child's life. Ever. And he'd never meant to risk hurting Molly, but Flynn couldn't deny he'd been daring their relationship down roads where it could.

Hell, Molly didn't need to waste breath being ashamed of him. Flynn felt an avalanche of shame every time he looked in a mirror. Pretty hard to earn her respect until he figured out how to ante up from his end…but right now, this exercise in beating himself up was going nowhere. He recognized that his character needed an overhaul, but all those big burning questions were just blurring in his mind. His head was splitting from a merciless headache, his eyes burning from lack of sleep.

He closed his eyes for a minute.

Just for a minute.

But when he opened his eyes—surely it was only a minute later?—everything was different. The total, eerie silence got to him first. Moments before he knew he'd heard Molly and Dylan giggling in the kitchen. His mind started registering other strange things. The lamps were off. Fuzzy gray dawn light reflected from the east window. Somehow an ivory blanket was tucked around him—except for his feet. He could see his bare feet sticking out from the end of the short couch. His stomach was growling hunger pangs, his neck cramped, but the monster-mean lack of sleep headache was gone—so completely that the wild thought pounced through his mind that somehow he'd slept around the clock like some nitwit baby.

Thoughts of nitwit babies had him yanking off the blanket and lurching to his feet in a panicked rush. He nearly knocked over a lamp. But where was Dylan? Where was Mol?

The only room he'd seen the night before was her living room, but figuring out the layout of the place was easy enough.

Past the kitchen was a hall. The bathroom was identifiable by scents alone—her apricot shampoo, her hand cream smell, the spritzy perfume she always wore. There was only one other room after that, and the door was partially open.

He hesitated, then poked his head in. Although the muzzy, murky light blurred all the edges, he could see well enough. He hadn't heard Molly moving furniture last night, but she must have. A bedside table had been pushed in front of her dresser drawers. The double bed was squished up against the wall, Dylan secured between the wall and Molly's body.

His gaze broomed the shadows, taking in the details in a single sweep—a digital clock reading 5:45 a.m. A bra strap hanging from a chair. Attic-style furniture—nothing matched—but there were silk roses in a vase, fringed curtains...and a fluffy white comforter—that she'd kicked off.

His gaze homed on her with the pull of a magnet. The baby was snuggled up in a mound of blankets. Not her. She was laying on her tummy, as abandoned as a wood nymph. Heaven knew she wore good-girl accountant clothes by day, but that sure wasn't what she slept in. The nightgown shone like satin, the fabric a caress that stroked from the dip of her spine to the cupping swell of her fanny. Her legs were bare, her hair tousled, and one skinny nightgown strap had worked its way down her arm, baring one pearl-white shoulder....

The instant Flynn realized his hormones were wide-awake and tuned to rock and roll, his conscience issued a stern order to get out. He'd located his two critical missing links. He knew positively they were both here, both safe. That ended his excuse for being anywhere near her bedroom.

Still, just because his conscience presumed he was up to no-good didn't make it so. He had a perfectly legitimate reason for stepping in closer. It was freezing in that back bedroom. He just meant to cover her up. That's all. That's it.

But he'd just bent down to pull up the white comforter when Molly suddenly half turned. His no-good eyes immediately pounced on the bodice of her silk nightgown. It was drooping. Unforgettably. Unignorably. Baring one full breast all the way to the raspberry tip. His no-good eyes remembered some manners and diverted their focus upward toward safer territory—relatively speaking. Her pale taffy eyelashes fluttered up, revealing luminously sensual eyes.

"Hi, you." Her voice was a husky whisper.

"Hi, you back." His voice was husky, too, but not exactly for the same reason. She was still half asleep, maybe three-quarters. His head understood that. But his heart understood that this was how Molly would be if he were waking up next to her. Warm and near-bare and real, with a smile still goofy with sleep and glad-to-see-him welcoming. "I didn't mean to fall asleep on you last night, Mol."

"Truthfully that was my plan. That you'd do just that. But I had hoped to get you fed before you crashed." She reached out to touch his hand, as if touching him, tenting their fingers together, were as natural as rain. But she still had that goofy, groggy smile. And she still didn't seem aware that the view just below her neck was turning his throat dry. "You sleep well?"

"Like the dead."

"Good. You were a cranky, unreasonable bear yesterday."

It was hard to find a comeback for that epitaph on his character. He tried the obvious. "I'm sorry."

"Don't be sorry. I know you were exhausted. And you weren't being mean to me. You were being mean to you. Judging yourself harshly, hanging yourself without a fair trial." She yawned sleepily. "Don't do it again."

"I...okay." This conversation started crazy and was just getting crazier. But when he tried to pull his hand free, intent on yanking up the comforter to block that vulnerable view of her, her fingers tightened their hold, squeezed warmly.

"Is it time to get up?"

"Nope. It's really early. You can go back to sleep, Mol."

"Your hair is sticking up. You look pretty silly."

"I just woke up."

"And you look like a wild warrior, fresh in from battle. Very sexy. Have you had a lot of women tell you you look incredibly sexy first thing in the morning?"

"Um, no." He cleared his throat. Vaguely he recognized that he was in hot water and sinking fast. Mol was going to seriously wake up any second now. Maybe he could sell her on the judicious reason he was in her bedroom to begin with, but he didn't want her embarrassed. She just didn't realize she was talking to him like...well, like lovers. Nonsense, silliness, intimate teasing. With the right man, it'd be different, but Flynn was too painfully aware that he wasn't on that "right man" potential lover list for her. "Mol, if you close your eyes right now, you'll go back to sleep and be able to catch another full hour of zzz's."

"Okay," she murmured, "only give us a kiss first. I can't sleep without a kiss."

Well, hell. He doubted she meant that. It sounded like a childhood line so mesmerized that it just spilled out in that half awake, half dream state she was in. But she was so close. And when he pulled the comforter up, thinking he'd just block temptation out of sight and then it'd be safe to kiss her. Once. Lightly.

He leaned down. That blurry smile of hers disappeared. Her eyes met his, touched his, and suddenly he wasn't sure if she were awake all this time or not. She'd looked at him that way before he'd kissed her other times—a little afraid, a little unsure, but that yearning and awareness electric between them like a lightning storm.

She lifted a hand, making that damned rapscallion comforter slip down again. Her fingers curled around his neck. Pulling him down. Pulling him to her.

"Da!"

Flynn jerked upright as if somebody'd slapped him.

The baby always woke up in a kick-ass frame of mind, ready to go and impatient to start the day's adventures. It had razored through Flynn's conscience before that the kid could have inherited that exhausting trait from his father's genes. But the tyke's vocabulary so far had been limited to "madoo" and "gabaloob" and other nonsensical sounds.

Flynn tried to console himself that Dylan couldn't possibly realize what he was saying. Only darn it…he actually seemed to. The baby promptly scooched free of the blankets and was already starting to climb on Mol. Over Mol. To him. And again he bellowed delightedly, *"Da!"*

Seven

"**M**ol! Shake a leg!"

"I'm coming, I'm coming..." Molly jogged into her kitchen in stocking feet. She'd dressed flustering-fast in her favorite navy blue striped suit, but she hadn't had time to put a face on yet, and she was still plugging in earrings. She stopped dead when she saw the spread Flynn had laid out for her. "Good heavens, I thought you were just going to make some coffee and feed the baby. You didn't have to go to all this trouble."

"Sure I did. I figured you needed a good breakfast for strength—since I personally know the slave driver you work for. And I owed you a thanks for letting us sleep over. Breakfast is served, ma'am—all I need to know is how you like your coffee."

"Black is fine." She wanted to chuckle at the state of her kitchen. Almost. Flynn must have seen something in her expression because he abruptly cleared his throat.

"Now I realize your kitchen looks like it needs a garden hose and shovel to recover, but just cover your eyes. I'll take care of that later. I had a little help putting this together."

"I can see that." She saw the baby, the room, the messes, but she also saw the devil-may-care glint in Flynn's eyes. It had taken her a long time to figure out that easy, wicked humor of his covered up a different man entirely. When Dylan called him "Da" earlier, Flynn had been as rattled as a buck caught in a hunter's spotlight. He'd looked panicked, but something raw and painfully vulnerable had been in his expression then, too. Not now. McGannon had defenses thicker than brick walls. He was back to joking, back to charm, and seemed determined to keep her too busy to bring up anything that happened earlier.

He hustled her into a seat, slapped a fancy omelet garnished with orange slices in front of her, then followed that up with a splashing hot mug of coffee. Someone had folded a napkin just so, decked out the table with the vase of silk flowers stolen from the living room and found her white linen table mats. Molly suspected it was the waiter—the one with the three beads of sweat on his forehead and a kitchen towel hanging drunkenly from his pocket.

Her oasis of formal dining was quite a contrast to the rest of the room. The smell of burned toast hovered in the air. Pans and cutting boards and debris were piled in her sink like a minimountain. The baby was on the floor on a blanket, eating Cheerios and toast and milk picnic-fashion. Judging from the state of the blanket, Molly guessed at least one mug of milk had spilled, maybe two. Most of the toast jam was on Dylan's face and sleeper. At some point earlier, a pint-size mouse must have gotten into her cupboards, because soup cans were still rolling on the floor.

"Wow, are you a big help, short stuff!" Dylan let loose a string of babble in response to this praise. Flynn interpreted it a little differently.

"The kid's a one-man demolition derby. In fact, I was thinking about this. All these centuries, I think we had a key to world peace that no one ever tapped into. Next time there's a war, don't send soldiers, just send kids in the one-to-two-year set. Bring an enemy to their knees in no time. You like those eggs?"

"They're beyond delicious..." But she'd barely swallowed one savoring bite before the telephone rang. She reached behind her for the wall receiver. The caller was her sometime-date Sam, who'd just nailed some free tickets for a Western University hockey game that night and wondered if she could go.

Talking to Sam was as easy as putting on a pair of bedroom slippers. Her concentration stayed focused on Flynn. He'd taken a long drink of her legs in the suit's short skirt, met her eyes with a look that could have kindled a forest fire and noticeably hadn't looked at her directly since. Of course, he was busy, jamming soup cans back into her cupboard while trying to stop Dylan from pelting him with Cheerios.

Still, he was clearly a mess, she mused. Not Dylan. Dylan was just making baby-type messes.

McGannon was the serious powder keg. They were going to ignore that almost-embrace in her bedroom, she figured out. Just as they were going to pretend Dylan had never said that emotionally loaded word "Da." And if he felt any awkwardness playing like a married couple, with the mom-dad-baby all trying to get ready for work at the same time, it didn't show. Heaven knew McGannon was exasperatingly perky and good-humored in the mornings, but he wasn't usually frantic-eyed and unshaven and chasing around so fast you'd think he was trying to catch his tail.

"Thanks, Sam. I'll catch you another time..." Molly hung up and reached again for her mug of coffee.

"So this guy's name is Sam..." Flynn dove a hand into his shirt pocket, came up with three Cheerios and sighed. "A good friend of yours?"

"Just a friend. Ran into him at a bank when I first moved here, found out he was a fellow CPA...Flynn, I don't think it has to mean some big monumental thing that the baby called you 'Dad.' He's just old enough to be trying out all kinds of words and syllables, but whether he actually even knows what that word means isn't automatically a—"

"So is this Sam a nice guy? I'm just asking because it sounded like you were turning him down about something. If he's giving you some kind of hard time..."

"Uh-huh." Not that Flynn was as subtle as a brick, but Molly didn't need a PhD to figure out they weren't going to talk about baby language and dad bonding—at least not right now. "Well, rest easy on Sam. He's very nice. In fact, I'm infamous for dating nice guys. It was almost a joke in my family. My two sisters used to bring home these adorable bad boys, gave our parents ulcers. Not me. I always brought home the same kind. Serious students. Clean-cut. Ambitious, hard workers, stellar futures ahead of them..."

She stopped to chuckle. Dylan had started crawling toward her cereal cupboard—until Flynn, faster than a football tackle, had thrown himself on the floor with his back blocking the cupboard door. He reached up for his coffee mug, scarfing down several sips with an eagle eye peeled for the baby's next move. "So how come you didn't marry any of those saints?"

"I don't know, but it's sure worrisome. Every woman I know complains she can't find a good guy. I find a pack of 'em, darn near Wonder Men, and not a single one of them rang my chimes."

The devil's eyes flashed with humor—and something else. "Maybe those saints were boring you to death?"

"Maybe."

But the humor almost immediately faded from his eyes...possibly because the baby chose that moment to climb onto his chest and push a nice, sticky piece of toast down his shirt. "Well, you just stick with those saints anyway, Mol. Keep your standards high. Chime-ringing's no proof of anyone with staying power."

"We're talking some pretty heavy philosophy for a man whose entire neck is covered with grape jam," Molly said wryly. "And how come I'm the only one getting grilled here? It's your turn to ante-up with a little history."

Flynn winced. "My past love life's a little sore point right now for the obvious reason. I'd rather talk about how to get grape jam out of shirts. I've tried a couple of cups of bleach—"

"Skip the bleach. Buy strawberry jam instead of grape." Molly carried her plate and silverware over to the counter and opened the dishwasher.

"That only sounds like a brilliant solution on the surface. He loves grape."

"I could rashly suggest that you say no to the baby, but that'd be a waste of breath. Forget that and just buy more shirts, tough guy. I'm your accountant, so I happen to know you can afford it. And you happen to be conveniently ducking the question about your love life—"

"How did we ever get talking about this subject to begin with?"

"Who knows? Who cares?" Efficiently she started making short work of the dishes. "Every woman in your life couldn't have been like Virginie. Sometime you must have been in love."

"Well, sure. At last count I'd been in love a couple hundred times."

"McGannon! I meant the kind that lasts *after* the first cataclysmic clash of hormones."

"Oh. Well, there was a girl my junior year in college. Shannon Rivers. For the record, she was no beauty, kind of chunky, big glasses...but there was something about her that gave me flu symptoms, couldn't eat, couldn't sleep. When she was around, nobody else was in the world that I noticed. Offhand, I'd say it was that messy, troublesome, extremely tiring kind of love you're talking about...."

"Yeah, those are the symptoms," she said wryly.

"We moved in together for a while. But then I got called home for a term, a family problem. By the time I got back to school, we drifted apart. Which is probably just as well. She was already seeing kids and furniture and mortgage payments in our future."

Molly glanced at him. She wasn't sure why she kept pursuing this conversation—both of them had handled it light and teasingly, but beneath the surface were subjects that made her uneasy, awkward. Still, for the first time since she'd known Flynn, he was revealing chunks of information about himself she hadn't known before, and it mattered. Somewhere there had to be a reason why he was afraid of the baby, afraid of being a father, afraid of marriage, for that matter. She grabbed a dishrag. "It must have been quite a problem for you to have to leave school for a whole term?"

"Just something that happened. No big deal."

She guessed it was. She guessed it was one big huge hairy deal in his life, because Flynn met her eyes squarely, honestly. The big lug was as self-aware as a slab of granite. He didn't seem to know the look in his eyes was as haunted as old pain. "You decided that early in life that you didn't want kids, marriage, all that traditional future stuff that everybody else was hot for?"

"I didn't own a lamp, Mol. Didn't know if I could make a living. Didn't have a clue where I was headed."

"Who does, in school?"

"Yeah, well. I got this wild idea growing up, that nobody should make promises they weren't damn sure they could keep."

Again she looked at him. Something inside her turned velvet-quiet on the inside. Her voice was gentle. "Someone made you those kinds of promises, McGannon? Someone who really let you down?"

He ducked that smoother than a cardshark in a poker game. "If you're looking for deep waters to analyze, you're gonna be mighty disappointed. The truth is more like, I tend toward selfishness. I'm a technology slob, work all hours of the day and night, never mastered the art of tact—as you know. I squeeze the top of the toothpaste, drink milk from the carton. Now, who'd want to live with me long-term? Hell, I have a tough time living with me."

Well, Molly mused, he had part of that right. She understood he meant to joke—maybe even to jokingly warn her away from becoming involved with him. But Flynn *did* seem to have a tough time living with himself, ever since the baby had shown up in his life. "Damn," she said suddenly.

He'd just lurched to his feet in chase of Dylan aiming for her pots and pans when he heard her swear. "I know, I know, I see where he's headed. I've got duct tape all over my kitchen—which hasn't worked worth beans. I'm thinking of padlocking all the cupboards next."

"I wasn't swearing at your angel, McGannon. He can have all my pots and pans as far as I'm concerned. But I just glanced at the clock. I'm going to be late for work if I don't hustle."

Flynn scratched his chin. "Um, honestly, love, I'm pretty sure you don't need to worry that the boss'll complain if you're a little late."

Her heart heard that "love." For two seconds, her pulse picked up a winsome, keening feeling—but of course she realized he was teasing; she'd known for a blue moon that word was no more than lip service for Flynn. "What the boss does and what I do are two different things. My job's getting payroll out on time on Friday...."

She jogged into the living room, came back hopping as she pushed on shoes and bent down to kiss the baby. "Goodbye, lovebug, I'll see you later. And as for you, McGannon—you can use anything you find in my bathroom, but do *not* squeeze the toothpaste from the top or you die."

He was still chuckling when she left. So was she, but traffic was jammed on Westnedge, and en route to work she glanced at the rearview mirror. That quick glimpse of herself made her pause.

She was still only wearing one earring. Hadn't put on a lick of makeup. Her hair looked more tumbled than brushed, her cheeks were flushed, her eyes brighter than Christmas tree lights. Being around McGannon was dangerous. She'd never—never—shown up at work less than professionally put together.

It went against her entire fastidious, fussy grain. And the blooming flush on her cheeks scared her.

Those fears were still spinning in her mind as she chased in the office door, yelled good mornings at Ralph and Simone, and then closed herself up in her neat, organized, safe office with all her neat, organized files around her. Burying herself in routine should have helped. It didn't. She was crazy about statistics, but no horrendously complex set of figures could distract her this morning. Not from thinking about Flynn.

Increasingly Molly realized how alone he was, on the inside, the outside, all ways. And it really seemed that he was turning to no one for help with Dylan. Except her.

She wasn't sure yet if Flynn had lost his way because of the baby. Or was finding his way because of the baby. Either way, he was on a major life course change that wasn't about her. It was about him, figuring out his life and what mattered to him, problems no one could resolve but him.

Molly couldn't *not* help. How could she ignore that vulnerable baby? And she was just coming to understand that that two-hundred-hefty-pound wild-haired redhead was even more vulnerable. But it was her heart that risked being twisted in a wringer when this was over. Nothing Flynn said ever indicated he even believed in love—much less that he saw or wanted her in any permanent way in his life.

She simply had to quit this. Quit falling in love with him. Just push a stop button and get tough on herself.

She could help him with the baby and still keep a distance.

Because she had to.

* * *

Ten days later Molly pulled in to the office parking lot after lunch. Simone was just climbing out of her car at the same time. "Can you believe this pagan climate?" Simone groused. "Snowing—and it isn't even the end of October!"

"I know! Grab a hand before we both kill ourselves." Molly hooked an arm around Simone to keep them both from slipping. Snowflakes had been drifting down before lunch, but the weather had deteriorated to a hard-driving sleet in the last hour, and suddenly the parking lot was a skating rink. Neither woman wore boots, and they both slip-slided to the door and were shivering hard by the time they stomped inside. "I'm afraid the roads could really be bad by tonight."

"You heard the weather forecast this morning? Partly sunny, chance of rain," Simone said dryly.

"I think weather reporting is an ideal job. Where else can you get paid well for being dead wrong?"

Simone chuckled. "I'm going to grab a cup of hot tea before heading for my desk. You want one?"

"Maybe a little later. I don't hear either of our resident redheads yelling at the moment, but I was going to swing by and check on Dylan for a couple of seconds—"

"Now there's a surprise," Simone murmured wryly. "The whole place has become attached to that baby, but you're the worst, Molly."

"I'm not attached—"

"Uh-huh." Simone never argued with anyone, except about work. "That man's got himself caught between a rock and a hard place. And I can't believe the baby's mother hasn't even tried to contact him again."

Neither could Molly. Flynn, being Flynn, had been frank with all the staff. They all knew Virginie's name, and that he'd had DNA test for paternity a week ago. Even if Flynn hadn't been bluntly honest by nature, it wasn't like he could hide the problem of Dylan.

The entire office had turned into a giant nursery. Molly strode past Brainstorming Central, unbuttoning her coat, her cheeks were still burning, her toes still unthawed. She stopped to pick up a baby shoe, then a push-pull toy with bells and whistles that everyone had been tripping over for a week. Ralph had brought in drums—which the baby loved—but no one was speaking to Ralph.

She said a quick hello to Bailey, then poked her head into Flynn's office...and abruptly tried to back out. She hadn't realized there was anyone in there with him.

"Mol, come in. I want you to meet Gretchen Van-Houser."

"I didn't mean to interrupt—"

"You're not interrupting. Gretchen's just putting her coat on—we're done here, but she's going to start tomorrow as Dylan's nanny."

Molly quickly stepped in to shake hands. She knew he'd been interviewing baby-sitters all week. There was no chance he could continue running the business with a baby in tow, but none of the interviewees—at least until this one—had come close to pleasing Flynn. "It's nice to meet you," she said warmly.

They only chatted for a minute before Flynn walked Gretchen to the exit door, but he signaled Molly that he wanted her to stay. She curled up on the carpet with Dylan, playing with his roly-poly ball, until Flynn walked back in. "So what'd you think?"

"Well, I only had a few seconds with her, but she looked fine. And right away, I could see Dylan was taken with her." Molly had liked the girl on sight. She was young, fresh-faced and sturdily built, wearing a teddy bear sweatshirt and jeans. Her long brown hair had been simply pulled back, her eyes warm and friendly.

"Yeah, slugger took to her like a duck to water. She's going for an elementary teaching degree, dropped out for a term to earn some money. But maybe she's too young?" Flynn rubbed the back of his neck. "Hell, I don't know why it's so hard to find the right person."

"Um, McGannon. A few of us have tried to mention that you have a couple of unusual ideas about nannies," Molly said delicately. Flynn saved the roly-poly ball before it disappeared under the desk and plunked down next to her. Maybe it was her imagination that the office temperature suddenly rose ten degrees. There was nothing but humor in his eyes as he watched her playing with the baby in her herringbone suit and heels.

"Like what's so unusual?"

"Like most baby-sitters expect to work out of a house, not set up baby care in an office."

"Well, hell. I'm supposed to trust a total stranger with the kid, when I can't be around to make sure everything's going okay? I don't think so. I'd rather they were right here where I can keep an eye on 'em."

"You don't think Dylan's a little young to read the classics to? That possibly he isn't quite ready for listening to violin concertos? Tapes on mathematical theory?"

"Now, Mol, the kid's had a rough start. A lot of upheaval. He needs some advantages to even the scale. And I read all these parenting books and studies on IQ. If you expose a kid to music and books and arts at a young age, they tend to…"

Molly didn't mean to tune him out, but she'd heard all this before. So had the staff, until they were glassy-eyed. Flynn never lacked for enthusiasm, but he used to wax on excitely in staff meetings about some virtual reality application for a new software product. These days theories on parenting theory were strewn all over the place, and he could go off on a solo aria about teething at a moment's notice.

She felt hopelessly charmed by his bond with the baby...and increasingly hopelessly confused why Flynn didn't seem to see it himself.

Today, though, something else was going on with him. She could sense it. She could even see it. His disgracefully threadbare black T-shirt showed off the tense, tight muscles in his arms and shoulders. He was too wound-up to sit still. A shock of hair brushed his temple; he kept slicking it back, and electric energy just seemed to vibrate from those sexy eyes of his. He hadn't touched her since the evening he'd spent the night. But it was there, chemistry in a simmering beaker, every time he looked at her. For weeks now—maybe months—she'd been trying to pretend that smoke would just go away if she ignored it.

"Molly?" She swiftly banished those thoughts when she heard the sudden change in his voice. He was through ranting on about baby theories, and his tone turned low and quiet, his gaze oddly intent on her face. "I didn't ask you to stay just to talk about Dyl's new nanny. I found out something an hour ago, and I need to tell you—"

The telephone jangled on his desk. He glanced up impatiently. "Just stay one more minute, would you? Whatever this is, I'll take care of it quickly. I—"

When the phone jangled again, he lurched to his feet and grabbed the receiver. He wasn't on the phone a full minute before Molly realized that the caller was some member of his family...and that Flynn had gotten the results of his paternity test back.

Eight

"**I** didn't mean to scare you by leaving a message on your machine, Mom. There's no emergency, nobody hurt. I just couldn't reach you this morning and there was something I needed to tell you..."

Molly felt unsure whether to sit tight or bolt for the door. Flynn had asked her to stay, but that was before he realized the caller was his mom. The last thing she wanted to do was intrude on a personal family conversation. But Dylan—in that single instant when both adults had taken their eyes off him—had abandoned his roly-poly ball and taken off toward the executive bathroom.

Molly scrambled to her feet and pelted after him. Dylan liked bathrooms a little too well. Last week, in fact, he'd managed to unravel an entire roll of paper and stuff it into the toilet. She scooped up the urchin, closed the bathroom door and settled him on the carpet again with baby blocks, thinking that Flynn couldn't possibly have a serious conversation and baby-sit their resident terrorist at the same time.

But she didn't stay because of Dylan. Or even because she quickly realized from the conversation that he must have gotten the results of his paternity test back. She stayed because Flynn was suddenly so quiet, so still—so totally unlike the McGannon she knew.

"Mom, sit down. No, no, like I said, this isn't a crisis or any emergency. It's just…sit down for me, okay?"

He'd half turned in his office chair. The bleak, blustery day only let in murky light through the windows, but his computer lamp was switched on. His profile was stark in the light, his shoulders as stiff as stone, his jaw profiled at a proud angle. He was hurt, she sensed. His face was as familiar as sunshine and rain, and he typically barreled through life spilling emotions right and left. But not pain. She'd never caught him with an expression that revealed any kind of personal hurt.

"…I don't know another way to tell you this but straight out. Mom—you have a grandson. His name is Dylan. He's a little over a year old…now, take it easy, take it easy, one question at a time. No, I didn't suddenly get married. I'm not married to the child's mother, or going to be. Yes, I…"

Dylan crawled over to her coat, absconded with her scarf and took off with it to his hammock. He plopped in with a chortling giggle, clearly counting on Molly to give chase. But then he yawned. Molly could have sworn Flynn wasn't even aware of the baby, yet without looking, instinctively, he reached out a hand to start the hammock swinging.

"…Yes." His voice was so clear it sounded vulnerably naked to Molly. "I got her pregnant…and you're absolutely right, there are no excuses. I realize how it sounds like dad, but I wasn't trying to hide any truth from you or deny this happened. I honestly didn't know until recently that you had a grandson or that I was a father...."

Something changed in his eyes when he mentioned his dad. Molly didn't know what the reference meant, and she kept telling herself to leave—she could just pick up the baby, take him upstairs; Flynn couldn't have meant for her to stay and hear an intrusive personal conversation like this. But damn him. His face had turned gray, his eyes old.

That he hadn't told his family about Dylan before this troubled her. Molly had just assumed he'd told his clan the story from the time Virginie walked into his office. She couldn't imagine keeping such a huge, traumatic secret from her own family. They could hardly offer help if they didn't know.

Yet the longer she listened, the more her stomach clenched in an aching fist. Flynn hadn't asked for help before. And it was more than clear that he wasn't asking—or expecting—support from his family now.

"...Yes, this is a for sure. The baby's right here with me. And I don't know how I could have done such a thing, either...yes, I realize that's traditionally the right thing to do, but there is no chance of my marrying her, Mom—none, zero, that's not going to happen...I'm not calling to ask you for anything. I just called to tell you that you have a grandson. Whatever you're thinking about me because of this—I assumed you'd want to know. And want to see him..."

There were long silences between his comments, but it wasn't hard for Molly to realize he was being crucified. His dad's name came back into the conversation, and again Flynn's jaw locked at that rigid angle. Molly couldn't help but think how her own parents would have responded to such news. They expected responsibility from her, and she knew they'd be disappointed, upset, but no matter what her age or the problem, she never doubted they'd come through to support her if she needed them—and vice versa.

Obviously everyone wasn't blessed with her kind of close family. Or possibly his mom initially responded emotionally to a problem—Molly told herself not to draw judgmental conclusions when she really knew nothing at all. Yet she couldn't help noticing that Flynn shouldered the problem without offering explanations or excuses. He never revealed Virginie's name, or that Virginie had lied to him about birth control, never mentioned that just possibly it took two to make this kind of mistake—or that he wasn't the first man since kingdom come to get a woman pregnant. He never attempted to defend himself in any way.

Finally, though, he said, "Mom, I understand how upset you are…but you're upset with me, not the baby. If you and Dad want to come for a visit to see Dylan…"

When another little silence followed, guilt caught up with Molly like an unpaid parking ticket. Her eavesdropping this long was really unconscionable. She slipped off her shoes, grabbed them and her coat and tiptoed toward the door—unfortunately just as Flynn hung up the phone. His office chair creaked as he spun it around to face her.

Warmth flushed her cheeks. "Flynn, I'm sorry, I didn't really mean to stay once I realized that was a personal call."

"Well, that's a two-way street. I wouldn't have asked you to stay if I'd known it was coming—and that conversation was about as much fun as a root canal. But one way or another, you must have figured out what I wanted to tell you."

"Yeah, you got the paternity tests results back." She hesitated. Discovering positively that the baby belonged to him was the major thing on his table, but somehow she just couldn't pretend she hadn't heard that conversation. "Flynn, you really never called your family about Dylan until just now?"

His eyebrows arched. "There was nothing to tell them—until I knew for sure if Dylan was their grandson."

"Nothing to tell them?" Oh, hell. She stashed her coat and shoes on his chair again. She'd already been caught intruding. A little more was just a difference in degree. "You had a giant problem you were coping with on your own, McGannon. They wouldn't have helped you?"

Again the question seemed to startle him. "I would never have asked them. I'm thirty-five, Mol, not an eighteen-year-old boy. For a lot of years here, they've brought their worries to me, not the other way around. And we just had some extra circumstances in my family. I can't even remember bringing a problem to my mother. She needed to be able to depend on me. Anyway..."

Flynn lurched out of his chair as if he were in a hurry to cut off that whole subject. Molly wasn't. Maybe she didn't understand what those 'extra circumstances' were, but she had a sudden bleak picture of a very young Flynn with those very old eyes. A boy who'd developed pride in turning to no one. A man who felt shamed if he had to.

"Anyway..." Flynn said "...that's water over the dam. The kid's mine. He's the only problem that matters." He looked down at the baby. Dylan had dropped off, his thumb in his mouth, Molly's silk coat scarf clutched in his other hand. "I guess I knew before this. The red hair, the bad temper, the streak of gambler in him—he really does love danger. Anyone that mite-size who could cause this much trouble had to inherit that stuff from some-where."

"You love him, Flynn," Molly said softly.

He lifted his head. "A set of genes doesn't make any-one into a decent father. I still don't know what the right thing to do is, Mol. Nothing's changed."

He was too big to strangle. She swept over and kissed his cheek instead. Even as she surged up on tiptoe, she realized it was a stupid move. But McGannon was being stupid, looking so rock-stubborn and angry and lost, so blind about himself that he couldn't see the reality of how much he'd changed—how much he was changing—if someone slapped him in the face with a mirror.

Her lips just whispered on his cheek. Lingered barely long enough to imprint his scent, his texture in her head, yet her pulse was suddenly rushing, rushing, like a hot moving river. She withdrew, backed down from her tip-toes. But Flynn caught her wrist and held it for a long moment. That swiftly, the expression in his face changed. Nothing in those magnetic blue eyes had anything to do with the conversation about his mother.

"What was that for, Mol? I didn't do anything to earn that kiss."

The way he looked at his baby had provoked that im-pulsive kiss. He loved Dylan. She'd been exasperated that he couldn't see it, touched at the way he showed love without even knowing it. But somehow this wasn't about the baby anymore. This was about them, and enough lightning between his hand and her hand to power a small country or two. "You think you have to earn affection? Sometimes kisses are free."

"I don't want kisses from you or anything else if you're feeling sorry for me."

"McGannon! Pity is the last thing I feel for you, you

dimwit! You made your own bed, as far as the baby, as far as your life. Where the Sam Hill did you get the idea that I felt sorry for you?"

Any *normal* man froze up when a woman yelled at him. Bewildering her completely, the tension in his shoulders eased and he loosened the killer grip on her wrist. Still, he seemed to hesitate. "Molly—don't gamble on me," he said quietly. "I'm a bad risk. I'm not sure what your feelings are, but I never could bluff in a poker game. All I have to do is touch your hand to feel a clawing from the inside out. Don't kid yourself that you can count on me to pull back if you start something."

She heard a distant phone ring. She heard Bailey bickering with Ralph as the men passed by the office. She heard Flynn warning her in a velvet-gentle baritone that they were going to make love if she risked any more impulsive kisses with him.

She wanted to say that he was sure making a mountain out of a molehill-size kiss. Only she'd had the same response to that molehill-size kiss. And her shaky knees and sea-wrecked nerves were nothing she could seem to immediately deal with. She bent down to pick up her coat and jam on her heels. "So your parents are coming this weekend?"

"Are we rather abruptly changing the subject, Ms. Weston?"

"Yup."

He searched her face, then let it be. "Yeah, they're coming. They live in Detroit. Mom said they'd drive up Saturday morning, won't spend the night, but they'll be here for afternoon and dinner. Maybe my sister, too."

"So what time do you want me over to help clean up the house?"

His bushy eyebrows raised in surprise. "I don't," he said bluntly.

"You don't want any company to help with this visit?"

"No. This isn't your problem."

"I agree completely. It isn't. But I'm not anteing anything in this particular poker game but an offer to push a vacuum and maybe throw something in a Crock-Pot. If there's something dangerous in that, I sure can't see it."

"I can. This is nothing I want you exposed to. I appreciate the offer, but forget it, Molly. I mean it."

When Flynn answered the door at nine o'clock on Saturday morning, he had Dylan on one arm, and the bucks in his other hand to pay the paperboy—who he assumed was the one laying a persistent finger on his doorbell.

With her hair yanked back in a ponytail, no makeup and wearing loose jeans and a bulky sweatshirt, Molly didn't look much older than said paperboy. But that ended the resemblance. Her cheeks were flushed, a woman's nerves in those big, soft eyes, and no male born filled out a pair of jeans the way she did. She was trying to juggle a bulky tote and carry a huge yellow Crock-Pot at the same time.

"Yeah, I know you told me not to come. But don't give me a hard time just this second, okay? This Crock-Pot is heavy. It's a French *Bourgogne* stew—not gourmet, but it's a pretty good company dinner. And I started it early, so all you have to do is plug it in. It'll be ready anytime after three, although it won't hurt to just keep it simmering until whatever time you want to serve. Hi, lovebug."

The "Hi lovebug" was for Dylan—who also got a kiss on his forehead—and then Molly flashed past both of them and aimed for the kitchen. When she emerged from there, her hands were empty. She started peeling off her coat, still talking nonstop.

"I've got one more box to bring in from the car. Cleaning supplies. I'd appreciate it if you'd carry it in—it's heavier than lead." She pushed her bangs off her forehead as she pivoted around, her gaze swiftly circling the room. "God. I had a feeling the place'd look like marines had camped here. Babies just have a knack for taking out a place. Frankly it'd just be easier if you stay out of my way. I'm a fussy neatnik—which you already know. Just point me to your vacuum and then go off somewhere— honestly, you don't even have to talk to me—"

He assumed she'd have to catch a breath sometime, but apparently not. So he tried interrupting, "Molly—"

Those eyes flashed, and that delicate chin suddenly stuck out with the posture of a belligerent bull dog's. "Look, McGannon. You've done a lot for me. I don't mean giving me a job—I'm a damn good CPA, could have gotten a job anywhere. I mean personally. You hired on a quiet little mouse, took me on, goaded me into figuring out how to speak my mind and stand up for myself. Now you don't get all the credit for corrupting me. I'm the one who did all the work of changing. But I think it's pretty darn mean not to let someone pay back when they owe you."

Flynn had known before this that he was suffering from character flaws. But not that he'd sunk so disastrously that he could fall head over heels—just for the look of a woman's bulldog chin. "Mol—"

She threw up her hands. "All right, all right. I admit there's more to it. You were right about my gambling on you. I'd worked myself up into a self-righteous huff, thinking you were sure giving me a hard time over an innocent kiss. Only it wasn't innocent. I haven't had a single innocent thought since I met you, McGannon. I knew perfectly well that I was inviting fire…and that maybe I wasn't so sure about anteing up if you'd called my bluff. Cripes, I *hate* it when a woman teases like that and now I've done it myself. So. The very *least* you can do is let me make it up to you by cleaning your house before all your company comes—"

"*Molly*—"

"Look, you can kick me out before your parents get here if you don't want me around then. And you don't even have to talk to me now. What's the big deal? I'll just spruce up the place a bit, help you set up a little dinner—"

"Weston, would you shut up for fifteen seconds?"

But her mouth was already open to answer that. So he stalked over, baby and all, and plastered a kiss on her parted lips. Her lips were smooth, crushably soft, and as chilled as the frosty morning outside—until his warmed them up. Her response stirred him to hot and hard in five seconds flat, and he still felt that way when he lifted his head. "I love you, Molly," he said lowly.

He saw vulnerability shine from her eyes, saw her swallow. But her voice came out thick with humor. "Uh-huh. Like you love toasted almond ice cream." She hesitated. "You're not going to give me a huge argument for showing up when you told me not to? I figured you would. I figure you didn't have the brains God gave a turnip, especially where your pride's concerned."

"This wasn't about my pride."

"No?"

"That was about not wanting to expose you to an awkward situation with my family. I don't want you hurt."

"You figure my doing some vacuuming and dusting is going to hurt me?" Since Dylan was making lift-me motions, Molly hefted him into her arms. "Look, I realize this isn't going to be an easy family get-together for you. Also that an outsider being around could make that even touchier. But it's not like I'm a stranger to the whole baby/Virginie problem, Flynn, and I think I could help. You have the baby to contend with while they're here. If you need to do some serious talking with your mom and dad, I can take charge of Dylan."

"No," Flynn said.

"No? I give you mountains of common sense and logic and all you can say is no? Where did we get him?" she asked Dylan. "I think we should send him back to the guy factory and see if we can get a different model—one with a heap less macho pride and testosterone."

"Read my lips, Mol. You're not staying. This is my problem, not yours, and I'm not dragging you into it."

Well, the damn woman. It was like trying to talk to a brick wall. She claimed she could read his lips just fine, but in the meantime the clock was ticking, he had company coming, and since she was already here, he'd be stupid to waste free slave labor.

His house did need a little spruce-up, but sheesh, the woman was a scrubbing fool. He didn't know anybody who washed behind the refrigerator, and why the Sam Hill would anybody move furniture to vacuum? Nothing he did was right. The whole place started to look strange and suffered a major invasion of girl smells—the wine aroma from that French stew, and furniture polish and disinfectants and the stuff she sprinkled on the carpet.

After a couple of hours of that, he was ready for a two-week vacation in Tahiti to recover. He didn't forget about kicking her out before his parents came. She just never let up long enough for him to do the kicking. First she scrubbed the place, then she scrubbed Dylan, and then she looked at him. He disappeared into the shower, emerged all clean, but that wasn't good enough. She ordered him back to his closet to find a shirt without a frayed collar or risk dire consequences.

Well, hell. When he came out with a shirt that finally pleased the shrew, she'd metamorphosed into dark green slacks and a cream sweater, every hair in place, makeup and perfume on. She looked energized enough to take on an army. He was so whipped from all the dadblasted housework that he could hardly think...but that didn't stop him from feeling.

Flynn couldn't explain how or why he suddenly realized how deeply, impossibly, painfully he was in love with her. All she did was stalk over with a scowl to straighten his shirt collar. There was nothing remotely sexual or suggestive in her touch, but something about her touch, her scent, her eyes, blasted him with a huge, engulfing wave of emotion. Suddenly he found it hard to breathe, hard to remember how he'd ever breathed without her.

Molly patted his collar down, stepped back—and then frowned all over again. "I don't know what you're thinking, McGannon, but you're making me nervous. Cut it out. We still have stuff to do—I don't know what your parents like to drink, and I haven't...holy cow, is that the doorbell? They couldn't be here already, could they?"

His parents had never been early in their entire lives, but they were today. Neither his parents nor his sister Therese had ever valued formality. They pushed the bell once, then turned the knob and poured in. His mom swooped in for a hug first, then his sister, with his father bringing up with rear with big, booming greetings.

His mother barely said hi before she demanded,

"*Where* is my grandson?" and then they all spotted Molly.

Flynn's stomach started churning acid. He'd never been afraid his clan would say anything directly to Molly that would make her feel awkward. His family was civilized—and God knew, they had decades of practice hiding problems from themselves as well as outsiders. Molly was just so sensitive. There was no way to prevent some real murky undercurrents from infecting this get-together, and he just didn't want her caught in the undertow.

At the beginning, though, things went okay. All the initial commotion made Dylan promptly start caterwauling at deafening volumes. Molly hustled over to the baby, so did his mother and sister, while Flynn attempted introductions through the confusion. Coats came off. Drinks got served. His son predictably filled a diaper, and two seconds after that was fixed, the baby discovered Therese's purse under a chair. Faster than anyone could spell trouble, the baby upended car keys, tissues, a tampon, change and a lipstick. His son—being his son—chose the most potential for disaster and took off with the lipstick at Olympic-crawl speeds. Five adults gave chase.

The baby thankfully broke the ice—Dylan could keep a houseful of adults busy without even straining himself. Eventually the women settled on the carpet by the fireplace, making female chitchat nonstop and keeping the baby entertained at the same time. Flynn kept watching Molly, who seemed to be getting on with his family like a house on fire.

He loved them. And hoped she might. He knew every strained dysfunctional seam in his clan's fabric, but those frustrations had never severed the bond he felt for family.

His mom, across the room, was chuckling at something Molly said. Ellen was fifty-five and no bigger than a shrimp. She wore her brown hair breezy-short and curly these days, and her tunic and leggings were typical of her casual clothes style. His sister had predictably gravitated right to the baby and was making faces to earn giggles from Dylan. Therese was thirty-two, and had their mother's same pipsqueak build and delicate bone structure. She'd gotten out of a rough marriage, and she'd started to look more and more like Ellen. Both his mom and sis were gregarious, loving and affectionate by nature—but both of them had older eyes than they should have, emotional scars that showed up in restless, darting gestures and jumpy energy.

His dad, by contrast, never showed a nerve. When the women engaged in their female chitchat thing, his dad plunked down next to him and started talking about a "big deal" that was going down. Flynn steeled himself not to comment. He couldn't remember a time in his life when Aaron McGannon hadn't been waiting for his luck to change, some ship to come in. What mattered more now was how Molly saw him. She had to notice how much he physically resembled his father. Aaron was big-shouldered, brawny-tall, with the same sharp cheekbones and mane of wild red hair. He could probably con a bottle from a baby, but that charm was real enough. He had a gift for making people feel at ease, had coaxed a giggle from Molly right off the bat with a wild compliment and an outrageous joke.

Dylan suddenly squalled and started fussing. Molly knew the signs and glanced up. "Flynn, do you want me to try putting him down for a nap?"

"I'm afraid the odds are ninety to one he won't go for it, but thanks, Mol, it's at least worth a shot. And looks to me like everyone needs fresh drinks." Flynn surged to his feet and aimed for the kitchen. Truthfully he needed a quiet minute alone. Just one would do. Things were going okay, but Flynn knew he could easily shoot off his mouth to his dad about Aaron's "new deal."

Blowing up at his dad had never accomplished anything. It was never Aaron's responsibility—always someone else's or "bad luck"—when the latest pie in the sky didn't cook. The problem burned Flynn like a raw sore, but his father showed no inclination to change, and his mom showed no inclination to leave him. The only thing Flynn had ever been able to do to make the situation better was to financially protect his mom by setting her up with a trust fund.

His mother followed him into the kitchen within seconds and closed the door. One glance at her face and he knew that quiet minute alone wasn't going to happen. "You want your usual? Cranberry juice?"

"I don't want a drink. I want a chance to talk to you."

"Yeah, I thought you would. But no reason I can't get you a drink at the same time." He clunked a handful of ice cubes into a glass and started pouring. Mentally he was already braced for his mom to vent some steam. Maybe he'd been waiting all the years from childhood—because those gentle, worried blue eyes had followed him like a hound when he was growing up. It never seemed to matter how many times Flynn proved she could depend on him; his mom had always feared he was his father's son, that the symptoms of weakness would show up—and win over his character—the way they had for his dad.

She saw his success in business as gambling. Hell, so did he. Nothing his mom had judged him for was ever wrong. He'd grown up with the same fear. It was the same reason he'd never married. The same reason loving Molly was forbidden. Nothing his mother could say to him was necessary—but that didn't mean his mom didn't need to get it out in the air.

"First of all, I like this Molly. She seems nice. Actually she seems more than nice. She's downright adorable. But she isn't the mother of your baby, Flynn."

"I'm glad you like her. She's a good friend. But she has nothing to do with the problem of Dylan—"

His mother leaned back against the counter and crossed her arms. "She could. If she's standing between you and any chance of your marrying the baby's mother."

"Well, you can whisk that thought right out of your mind. I told you straight the first time this came up—there's no chance of my marrying Dylan's mother. And Molly would be the last person on earth to interfere if that were a possibility. Mol's good—clear through to the bone, Mom. Don't even think about judging her or blaming her for anything. I'm the one you're ticked at."

"You're right. I *am* ticked at you." Out it came, in a furious rush. "I just don't understand any of this. How could you be so careless at your age to get a woman pregnant? Where *is* this woman? What's her name? How did all this suddenly happen so that the baby is with you?"

He couldn't answer all those questions at once. "Her first name is Virginie, and Dylan's here because she brought him to me."

"What's that supposed to mean? For how *long* is he going to be with you?"

"We haven't worked out any custody thing in a formal way yet. There hasn't been time—or opportunity."

"What kind of woman would sleep with you and then not tell you she was pregnant? What kind of woman were you involved with, for heaven's sake!"

"I honestly can't answer that—I don't know why she

didn't tell me she was pregnant from the beginning. We live in different states. But she tracked me down now, so she could have tracked me down then. She chose not to.''

"I didn't raise you to desert a pregnant woman, Flynn."

"I didn't. I wouldn't. I'm telling you honestly—I didn't know. But everything else you're saying to me, I've already said to myself. I've tasted every flavor of guilt. Still am. But I can't change what already happened."

"That's just the point. This shouldn't have happened. Damnation, at least your father only gambles with money. You gambled with a woman's life—and a child's. I taught you better. As much as I love your father, Flynn, you know how much heartache he's caused us all because of being a selfish, irresponsible dreamer. I never wanted you to turn out like him—"

Molly turned the knob and burst into the room in a bubbling rush. She stopped dead when she glanced at the two of them, and her face flushed. "I'm sorry, I didn't mean to interrupt anything. The baby went down for a nap—which struck me as a near miracle—and I thought we could eat if I just put a little hustle on dinner—"

"That sounds like a fine idea," Mrs. McGannon said briskly. "Flynn, you go out and talk to your dad and sister. Molly and I'll take care of putting dinner on, won't we, dear?"

"I'll stay and help." Flynn saw his mom flash a smile at Molly, which he trusted on a par with a politician's promise. He didn't want to leave Molly alone. His mother had obviously formed some opinions about Virginie's morals—and he just didn't want her thinking or venting anything like that on Molly.

"The two of us can handle it fine," Molly assured him.

"And really, you don't have to help, either, Mrs. Mc-Gannon."

"Nonsense. I never could sit still. Setting the table would give me something to do." The two women shared a glance. "You just go play host to the rest of the family, Flynn."

"Yup. You go, Flynn," Molly concurred.

Nine

Molly watched from the window as the McGannons piled into their car. Flynn had just walked outside to see his family off. Typically he hadn't thought to put on a jacket or shoes. A hurdy-gurdy wind was tearing through his hair, whipping at his shirt collar. The night had turned slate black, branches rustling in the shadows like wild secrets.

After all the commotion, the sudden silence seemed unnerving to Molly. Restlessly she rubbed her arms. She'd learned more than a few McGannon family secrets over the long day—not necessarily wild secrets, but unsettling ones. On the far wall, a ticking clock echoed the odd, edgy beat in her pulse.

Finally the car lights came on, and his parents backed out of the driveway. Flynn stomped back in, letting in a gush of bitter-cold air. "Molly?"

She put a smile on. Moved. "I'm in here. I was just going to clean up the last of the glasses—"

"Forget that, Weston." He showed up in the doorway, framed in firelit shadows. His face was ruddy, his eyes shining like wet jet—and honed on her. "Whatever dishes are still left, I'll do in the morning. You're all through working. Sit down and put your feet up. I'm going to get us a shot of the most potent thing I've got in the kitchen, check on the monster and I'll be back in two shakes."

Two shakes was too long. In the silence she heard that clock ticking again. She sat on the couch, bounced back up, sat back down, tugged on an earring. The huge fire Flynn built after the baby went to bed was roiling hot now. A log crashed in the fireplace grate, shooting sparklers up the chimney, making light gleam and dance on the white fur hearth rug, the forest green couches, the mullioned pane windows. The room couldn't have been more toasty warm, and still her fingertips were chilled.

She should go home, she thought. His parents had stayed later than expected. It was late, almost ten. She was whipped; so was Flynn.

But tangled pictures kept tumbling in her mind, replaying scenes from the long day. His dad was a charming, easy-to-be-with, hopelessly lovable darling—she'd never have guessed he had a gambling problem, if the women hadn't dropped so many hints that eventually the puzzle pieces fit in. Too many puzzle pieces. Flynn had obviously grown up with a mom and sis fretting that an apple never fell far from the tree, especially a male apple. His business success was incidental, his financial support and caring for them forgotten. Dylan was sure proof that Aaron's irresponsible and selfish genes had passed down to Flynn.

Go home, Molly. You have no excuse to stay. No matter

what you found out, there's nothing you can do about it. And yeah, she knew that, but her pulse kept rattling like that incessant clock, beating nerves, beating warnings that she was already too involved with him. Heart involved. Love involved. The complicated mix of caring and pain his family dished out made her hurt for him, with him. Too much so. Her female antenna was all tuned to the same radar—she felt too much now, for a man who'd never made a promise to her or even implied one. If she had a brain in her head, she'd leave.

But she was waiting when Flynn strode back in, carrying two brandy snifters. "I made yours short. I know you're driving. But I didn't figure a few sips would hurt. It was a long day."

"It turned into one," she agreed. "The baby sleeping okay?"

"Like a rock. He was so furious when I put him down that I figured he'd stay awake just to spite me—but I knew he was worn-out from the company." He crashed on the couch cushion next to her, leaned back his head and propped his stocking feet on the coffee table. "I expect you are, too. Did my mom give you the third-degree in the kitchen?"

"I liked your family, Flynn." She took a sip of the brandy. It slid down her throat like liquid heat, but did nothing to settle her nerves. The cushions sank under his weight, making her body naturally lean into his. Their shoulders touched, no more, but she couldn't be more aware of him if she swallowed a lightning bolt. The brandy splashed gold in the firelight, the same glow burnishing his face with shadows.

"Well, I'm glad you liked the family. It'll save my having to strangle 'em. But that didn't answer my question about how badly my mom grilled you."

"Not at all."

"Uh-huh. You can't lie any better than George W."
His stockinged toe reached over to nudge her stockinged
toe. There was nothing sexual in the gesture, nothing sexual in his whole attitude. He wasn't trying to inspire the
wayward thoughts tumbling in her head. Her mind seemed
to inspire them all on their own. "Pretty rough, was it?"

"Your mom was just being a mom, McGannon. She
loves you. They all do. Naturally she asked some questions. The news of a sudden grandson was bound to shake
them up...which means they were bound to be shook up
by any woman who was with you."

"That's exactly what I was afraid of—that they'd think
you were a cut from Virginie's cloth. And they'd say
something to make you uncomfortable."

She took one more potent sip of the brandy, then set it
down. "Neither your mom nor anyone asked me anything
I wasn't expecting. I think most families tend to poke and
pry if they get a chance. My dad was always a pistol—
any guy coming to pick up one of his daughters was lucky
if he wasn't exposed to a strip search and a lecture both.
And in case you forgot, I volunteered to stick around for
this visit."

"You didn't volunteer. You bullied and bossed me into
it."

She had. Because she sensed he needed her. And damnation, but she felt that antsy, restless kick in her pulse
again. One of these days he was going to figure out he
was crazy about his son, and that this whole full-fledged
crisis in his life was no crisis at all. He wouldn't need her
then, she understood—but he wasn't there yet. He *had*
needed her today. And her risky heart kept thumping the
drumbeat that he still did. "I told you before. You're the

one who gave me those how-to-bully lessons. Don't blame me if you don't like the consequences.''

"That's the point. That I didn't want you facing *my* consequences.''

"Flynn?''

"What?''

"Your dad gambles?'' she asked quietly.

That turned his head. She'd seen that expression on his face before. Bland. Closed in. Prepared to slough off anything serious rather than letting anyone too close. "Well, hell. I take it my mom aired out quite a bit of the family linen.''

"Some. Some I just figured out. But one of the things I couldn't figure out is why they take out his behavior on you instead of him.''

He hesitated. "Nobody does that. It's just…they love him. I love him. He's got a hundred great qualities. Smart—damn near brilliant in his field. Fun. Loving. Affectionate. But we gave up—all of us—believing he'd lick the gambling thing. He isn't going to change. You want some more brandy?''

"No, thanks.'' She hadn't finished the glass she had, which he could see. He obviously wanted the subject changed.

"Did I say thanks yet?'' He nudged her toe again.

"Nope.''

"Well, hell, why didn't you kick me? You know I'm an insensitive clod. The dinner was great, all that cleaning you did, putting up with the whole family scene—I owe you more than thanks. If I haven't told you recently, I love you, Mol.''

She'd heard countless "I love yous'' before from Flynn, knew it was a lip-service term for him. He meant affection. Nothing else. There was absolutely no reason why hearing it this time should inspire her to murder and mayhem.

But it did. It seemed like that ticking clock in her pulse had suddenly run out of batteries.

Flynn didn't do anything when she leaned forward. Possibly he just assumed she was getting up for some reason. For sure he wasn't expecting her to twist around and plop down on his lap. He was still sitting slouched, relaxed, his neck leaned back against the pillows—for a second. His head jerked forward abruptly, making it extremely easy to aim a kiss. Right where she wanted it.

He not only wasn't in the mood; for a moment she wasn't sure he was breathing. Initially he froze when she rubbed her lips against his. He stayed frozen for about as long as an ice cube in the tropics.

At last count, Molly was pretty sure she had somewhere around 4,387 inhibitions. She really didn't like loosening up, giving up control. She'd always felt like those inhibitions kept her safe from making impulsive mistakes... but now, she slid her fingers through his wiry, unruly hair and inhaled the texture of his smooth, mobile mouth. He tasted like a mistake about to happen—the kind of wicked, forbidden, unwise mistake she'd meticulously managed to avoid her whole life. He tasted like the only man who'd ever been worth that risk, and Flynn seemed to sample that flavor of temptation, too, because a groan rumbled out of his throat.

"Mol...what do you think you're doing?"

He was a grown man. She was quite positive he could figure it out. She nestled closer, aware he was becoming aroused because she could feel him, but also aware that his muscles were tense, as rigid as iron. She poured another kiss on him, this one softer, darker, deeper. For the first time all day, her pulse quit clanging anxiety. It was too late to worry. She was tired of worrying.

She was tired of pretending that she wasn't drowning in the deep end in love with him. She tilted her head, angling for a pressure cooker of a kiss this time, one that involved teeth and tongues. Flynn's hands clamped on her shoulders, but if he meant to stop her, that goal seemed to elude him. His warm, wet tongue met hers, touching, teasing, taking.

He'd kissed her back before. Not like this. Maybe he'd always been sexual dynamite for her, but it was as if he turned the steam up and the speed way, way down. She gulped a fresh lungful of air, submerged again, this time with her fingers on his shirt buttons. Another log crashed in the fireplace. Sparks whooshed up the chimney. His face looked painted with fire, his body heating as if he'd been long-distance running—when the only thing moving was her fingertips, over his collarbone, his throat, the springy hair on his chest.

"Mol—" His voice sounded scratchier than steel wool.

"Hmm?"

"I don't think you want this—"

"Yeah, I do."

"I'm not sure if you mean what you seem to be inviting—"

"Trust me. I mean it."

He lost his voice when she started pulling his shirt loose from his jeans. It took a moment before he found it again. "Did you have more than two sips of brandy when I wasn't looking?"

"Nope." She smiled, because he seemed to want her to. Then kissed him again. Long. Hard. Thoroughly. It went against her accountant's soul to neglect a detail. And there went his voice again, although he tried one more time.

"Mol, but if you're counting on me to say no...how about if you don't. If you're counting on my suddenly developing a noble streak...it won't happen. And—''

She wasn't sure what he needed to hear from her. She tried the truth. "I want you, Flynn."

Well, heavens. She wouldn't have thought those were particularly magic words, but either the words or her warbled whisper seemed to change everything. He claimed her mouth with dizzying pressure, pushed forward and lurched to his feet with her legs wrapped around his waist. They took the stairs that way, his carrying her, his kissing her. It was a dangerous way to travel. They careened off the banister once, off a dark wall another time.

He used an elbow to nudge open a door. The door slammed against the opposite wall; he used a foot to slam it back closed. The room was pitch-dark, impossible to see anything but shadowed furnishings, but a blast of frigid night air seemed to come from an open window. If Flynn normally preferred to sleep cold...that definitely didn't seem his intention tonight.

The bedsprings creaked when he dropped her on a long hard mattress, then followed her down. In the darkness her senses seemed acutely aware of textures—a rumpled feather comforter, smooth ice-cold sheets, pillows—yet every feminine nerve in her body seemed tuned only to Flynn. His scent. The building heat in his body. The black fire in his eyes, his rough-whiskered chin, as his mouth fastened on hers, leveling her into the mattress, claiming a kiss so wet and wild that she couldn't catch her breath.

He severed that kiss with a sound of frustration, then lifted her, long enough to pull the sweater over her head, then to swivel around and peel off her slacks and socks.

She heard his fingers, fumbling in a bedside table drawer for protection, then heard him skimming off his shirt and hurling it somewhere in the darkness.

He came back, then, for another kiss. His tongue plunged into the dark, wet corners of her mouth, seeking her tongue, finding it, taking it, arousing a hunger that scared and thrilled her at the same time. He knew. That kiss didn't end until he'd unhooked her bra and tossed it and her heart was beating like a runaway roller coaster.

"You're still wearing jeans," she hissed.

"Uh-huh. Because I'm smarter than I look. Is that how you thought this was gonna go, Mol? Fast and hot and over quick?"

"Yes. Now. Hurry."

He whispered, "No." Softer than a promise.

She didn't know what he was promising her. She didn't know what she expected. She hadn't thought anything beyond the driving and instinctive need to make love with him. All day that volcano had been building, fueled from watching his mom and sister judge him, triggered further when she grasped his dad's problem. It all added up to a painful lightbulb flash that Flynn never experienced the acceptance and family support she took for granted. He didn't know love. And for damn sure Flynn McGannon didn't love Flynn McGannon.

She couldn't change his history. Couldn't make up for anything, and their making love didn't solve a damn thing. She didn't care. Her heart knew it was right. Showing him how much she cared seemed a thousand times more important than any personal risk she was taking. Only suddenly she couldn't think. She'd been vulnerable countless times in her life before. But not like this. Nothing like this.

Her intent was to make him feel valued and loved, and no paltry mountain better try getting in her way.

Only the damn man kept goofing everything up.

They'd hurtled to near nakedness at rocket speeds. That hustling, urgent speed had sent excitement whistling through her feminine nerves in a heady, elemental rush. She needed that speed. She knew perfectly well she had those 4,387 inhibitions waiting in the wings to shake her up. Only Flynn had completely quit that charging pace.

And he was shaking her up. Deliberately.

The slow sweep of his palm down her bare skin burned. He brailled her in the darkness, learning her with his fingertips and his warm, wet tongue. He nipped the inside of her thigh, washed the inside of her navel with his tongue, cherished her breasts with his whiskered chin and tongue and silver-soft kisses. She was still wearing panties until he decided to remove them with his teeth. Slowly. Inch by inch, treasuring every patch of skin he exposed with more of those silky soft kisses.

She felt like a leaf sucked into his wild, lonely wind. Emotion poured from Flynn. Passion, prowess, an earthy savoring of everything to do with the act of loving— maybe she could have guessed those things, but not the loneliness, not the lovingness. The hunger in him was like an exploding dam, a pent-up need to give and share, not just to take.

They rolled. Her under him. Then her on top, so that his palms could caress the length of her spine, intimately cupping her fanny, and she could intimately feel the aching, hot arousal in his jeans. The comforter shifted and bunched every time they rolled, and she heard his rough, low laughter when they almost tumbled off the bed. A pillow got in his way; he hurled it—hard—a measure that heat and urgency were screaming in his pulse, too. Longing hissed through her. Desire like an electric ache that refused to be appeased.

It wasn't as if he inhibited her touching him in any way. He responded like lightning anywhere, anyhow she touched him, but he kept coming back for more of those daring, dueling, silver-soft kisses.

Flashes of light streaked through her mind. Not thought. More painfully acute shards of awareness. For a blue moon she'd known he was sexual dynamite for her, known she felt some elemental bond to him—even when her conscience had shot her clear, alarm warnings that Flynn was a dangerous risk for her. He could be insensitive, self-centered, selfish. She *knew* his faults. All the same things his family judged him for—his risking a child, his involvement with baggage like Virginie—she'd judged him, too.

But the man Flynn had been weeks ago was not the same man making love with her now. A complex and compelling man had been emerging in front of her eyes. And it wasn't just sexual dynamite taking her under in bed now, but a man experimenting with sensitivity. With unselfishly exploring her feelings.

With a cruel, ruthless determination to drive her clear out of her mind with wanting him.

"Flynn—"

"You're beautiful, Molly. More than beautiful," he said gruffly.

"Could you...?"

"Could I what, love?"

"Could you get around to taking off your jeans?"

"Soon," he muttered. "Eventually. We'll get to that, Molly Weston, but I have in mind loving you until you can't see straight first."

She unsnapped his jeans herself, since he was being

such a curmudgeon. That made him smile, and he smiled her a kiss. She could feel the curve of his lips on her temple, her jaw, trailing down her throat. He quit smiling when her palm slid inside his jeans. He was hard and fire-hot and her gentlest touch made him pulse alive.

"Uh-oh."

A gleam of black humor in his eyes. "Somehow I was hoping for a different response when we got this far."

"I'm just not absolutely positive this is gonna work."

"Trust me. It will. You're going to fit me—and I'm going fit you—so perfect that we just might spin right off the universe. You ready for a wild ride, love?"

She was seduced, long before he shucked off his jeans. Long before he wrapped her legs around his waist and took her with long, slow thrusts until she was as immeasurably a part of him as he was of her. It was his loving that seduced her, his cherishing, the caring he blessed on her with every touch, every kiss. Flynn showed her the depth of love, even if he never called it that. He showed her longing and belonging that bonded her to him like the missed part in her soul.

Her skin sheened and glowed. So did his. He whispered words of praise, words of demand to let go, for him, with him. The ride was as wild as he'd promised her, his thrusts building, building, until dark, hot firecrackers seemed to explode within, without, all through her. She called his name.

And in the darkness he hissed back, "Never, Mol. I'll never love anyone in this life like I love you."

Flynn woke up alone. His heart was pounding from a dream, a nightmare, that Molly was gone.

She *was* gone. Dusky dawn light filtered down from the skylight, revealing a room so empty he almost thought he'd dreamed her…dreamed making love, dreamed how she'd cleaved to him with all that open, giving, generous sensuality, dreamed her coming to him, with him, as if he'd found the lost half of his soul. It couldn't have been real. Molly wasn't his. Believing it a dream made more sense.

But his sleep-muzzy vision gradually cleared. Details came into focus. The comforter was tucked around him—only Molly could have done that, because he'd slept cold ever since he was a kid. Clothes were hurled everywhere. Her bra on a lampshade. His jeans on the gray carpet, her sweater on the black lacquer chest in the corner. The lacquered chest was the only nonutilitarian furnishing in the bedroom. He expected to wake up alone, never spent any time here until he unwillingly gave in to the day's exhaustion and crashed.

Molly was here. She had to be—unless she'd driven home naked, because all her clothes were still there. But the empty silence suddenly made him conscious of a distinctly absent noise factor. Dylan.

The terrorist always woke up predawn, always bellowed until Flynn raced in to fetch him. When the kid was ready to start the day, he was *ready,* and the monster had no appreciation for anyone's desire to sleep past six.

Only there was no sound of either the terrorist or Mol. Hustling out of bed, Flynn grabbed a robe and hiked into Dylan's room. It was hard to see anything through all the debris—damned room was like a cluttered toy store warehouse—but the crib was empty, no Dylan in sight.

He found them, downstairs in the kitchen. One look and suddenly he felt a clutch of nerves. He *wanted* her to be there. Only seeing her reminded him of exactly what they'd intimately and exquisitely done last night…and what they hadn't done.

"Well, good morning, lazybones. Dylan, will you look at what the cat dragged in?"

"Da!" Dylan, trapped in his high chair, saw him in the doorway and instantly reached out both arms, sending fistfuls of scrambled eggs in every direction. Flynn had to reach down to give him a kiss. The kid expected it.

Those long white legs of Molly's were still in his vision, though, mainlining hormones direct to his bloodstream. Apparently the breakfast in progress was scrambled eggs and sliced fruit and French toast. Molly was just pouring juice. She was wearing one of his shirts, which concealed her figure to midthigh. Her hair was mussed, her face scrubbed clean. The soft shadows under her eyes and whisker burns on her throat testified to exactly what she'd been up to the night before.

"Looks like you started breakfast without me," he said lightly.

"The big guy here doesn't seem to have a lot of patience in the morning. Something like his daddy, I was thinking."

He was thinking how perfect she looked, how easy it'd be to fast-scroll to a future full of the same pictures. Mol. His wife. Coming down to a disaster of a kitchen and her wearing his shirts. Maybe he'd throw away all her clothes so she had nothing to wear, ever, for the next forty years but his shirts. The pictures made his throat thick with more of those porcupine-sharp nerves...because he suddenly didn't know what Molly was anteing in this poker game. He only knew what he was.

She was smiling at him. But that welcoming smile had a little shyness, a little uncertainty. More the Mol she used to be. "Did you sleep well?" she asked him.

"Between the two of us, I don't think we got three hours total."

Her cheeks flushed and for a second, her eyes danced for him—but then she quickly, nervously turned away and busied herself pouring juice. "Well, I have to tell you, the only eggs left are on the cool side. You get up this late—I mean, for heaven's sake, it's six a.m.—and you can't be expecting anything but leftovers."

"I wasn't expecting...anything. Molly—" He dragged a hand through his hair, wishing to hell he knew the right thing to say and do. Hauling her into his arms and kissing her senseless was his first impulse. He loved her. Like he'd never loved anyone, like he never dreamed he could even feel. Imagining a future with her came more naturally than breathing.

But why she'd chosen to make love with him specifically last night suddenly mattered. She'd buckled his knees from the instant she'd snuggled on his lap—likely nothing would have stopped him from making love with her once he knew she was willing. Only he'd damned conveniently forgotten that her willingness directly followed the whole sticky family visit. They'd been rough on him. Justifiably, from his view. But it was just now occurring to him that Molly may have been motivated by sympathy, feeling sorry for him.

"What's wrong?" Molly asked quietly.

"Nothing. I'm just a curmudgeon in the morning." A flying wisp of scrambled egg hit him in the cheek. Dylan chortled, so did Mol...then so did he.

But he couldn't hold on to that chuckle, or fake a breezy mood. She plopped a plate of eggs in front of him, royal-fingered him to sit, then fetched a platter of French toast and plunked down opposite him. "Spill it, Mc-Gannon," she ordered briskly.

"The juice?"

"No, you doofus. Whatever's on your mind that's bothering you so much."

"I just...don't know if you're okay with this."

She seemed to translate through his bumbling stutter. Her eyes rested softly on his face. "I wouldn't have made love to you if I weren't 'okay' with it. More than okay." She hesitated. "Unless you regret it?"

"There's no chance in heaven or hell of my regretting it. None. But..." He knew she'd fallen for him. There was no other way, ever in this life, Molly would have made love with him without a serious love component for her. But however powerful and unforgettable their night together had been, Flynn was sharply aware that he had yet to earn her respect.

He grabbed a napkin, put it down. Hell, he never had known how to say anything but to blunder it out. "Molly, I don't know where you want this to go. And I don't know what promises you want or need from me."

Her eyebrows lifted. "Well, those aren't too complicated questions. Last night was never meant to be a noose around your neck. I wasn't asking for promises then, and I'm not now."

"You know my track record. You know I'm not sure what's going to happen with Dylan. You know what the family history is now, and the reasons I'm a risky bet as far as marriages or long term relationships—"

"Excuse me? Did I mention marriage?"

"No, but—"

"How about if you eat your eggs and we try this one step at a time, McGannon. I don't run around taking lovers, you know. I have in mind savoring the nice, illicit, wicked aspect of having you for a lover. Discovering you for a lover. Seeing where we can go with it. You have a problem with that program?"

"No."

"I don't have a crystal ball on the future. But if it stops working, last I noticed we were both adults. Either of us can raise a hand and call it off. As long as we're honest with each other, I don't see a problem. Now have we got that settled? Anything else on your mind?"

Yeah, there was. The damn woman made him love her even when she was fibbing straight to his face. Her bravado was as precious as her vulnerability. Flynn knew damn well that Molly was no woman to have an affair with. And that his lifelong fear of hurting someone else with his selfish, impulsive behavior...he'd never, never meant to risk that with her.

Yet he'd gambled last night. With her feelings. With her heart. And his own.

Flynn had yet to forget her feeling ashamed of him. And if sympathy motivated her making love with him, that emotion was the diametric opposite of what winning Molly would take. Her humorous claim about wanting a "wicked, illicit" affair was a fib of epic proportions.

She would never stay with a man she didn't respect. And Flynn knew he was on borrowed time to either earn that respect in her eyes. Or fail to.

Ten

Flynn was heavy-duty concentrating on a software problem when he heard the muffled, distant sound of Dylan's sudden high-pitched wail. He bolted out of his office chair and took the stairs two at a time to the upstairs conference room.

"What's wrong?" After hiring Gretchen two weeks before, he'd transformed the formal meeting room into a nursery.

Table and chairs had been replaced with play mats, mobiles, reading books, and close to every toy manufactured for the age-one set. Even in the middle of all the clashing colors and toy debris, though, he spotted Dylan on the floor—red faced and furious, caterwauling like a banshee…and Gretchen, kneeling next to him, making soothing noises. "What happened?"

When Gretchen spotted him, she smiled, but her shoulders stiffened defensively. "Nothing, really, Mr. Mc-

Gannon. He's just mad at me. Our little daredevil took off for the stairs. I was right there, and caught him before he fell. But he just didn't like it when I told him no.''

Dylan took one look at him and lunged. The shrieks turned off faster than a water faucet—a fair measure no one was killing him, no matter how convincing those pitiful wails had sounded—but Flynn didn't see he had any choice but to scoop him up. The thumb went into the mouth the instant Dylan was perched on his arm. "I'll take him for a while," Flynn told Gretchen.

Her smile died. "You don't have to do that, Mr. McGannon. I know you've got a staff meeting this morning. And honestly, we're doing fine. He'll get over being mad at me. He just doesn't like hearing that *no* word."

Flynn knew that—infinitely well—but Dylan was clinging tighter than ivy to brick. To put him down was to risk another temper tantrum. It wasn't like anyone in a five-mile radius could think when the kid was crying. At least he couldn't.

"I've got him. Don't worry about it. You just take a break and relax," he told Gretchen, and carried the slugger back down to his office.

The baby removed his thumb long enough to chortle, "Da!" sounding as thrilled as if he'd won the lottery. Well, one of them was happy. So far, Flynn's day had been a tornado of disasters and showed no signs of improving.

A blustery wind thwacked branches against his office windows, echoing his own rattling mood. He wasn't prepared for the upcoming staff meeting—three new accounts, and he had no strategy plan for any of them. Bailey had popped in earlier, bringing him a software dilemma—and God knew, if Bailey in his lucky bathrobe couldn't solve something, the problem had to be dicey.

Flynn traditionally loved impossible problems, but not when he couldn't concentrate. He couldn't concentrate because he was short on sleep. Dylan was getting a couple of new teeth. Pacing the floors in the middle of the night was the only thing that seemed to console him.

All that pacing and rocking had given him endless time to think about Molly. Guilt, as sharp as a knife blade, had been stabbing his conscience ever since they'd made love. No man—no good man—made love with a woman like Molly unless certain things were right. Hairy things. Like commitment. A possible future.

Sex so hot it burned the sheets was nice. But only marginally relevant. Molly had no reason to hook up with a lousy gamble like him unless—he figured—she saw some real transformation. She had to *believe* he'd changed. She had to see it.

He'd been wearing button-down shirts, Dockers—even socks—for two weeks now. Sold his Lotus, picked up a respectable-family-image Jeep Cherokee. The basketball hoop and putting tee had been removed from his office, replaced with banker chairs. He'd quit thundering at Ralph, quit telling off-color jokes to Bailey, tried to run the staff meetings at a more subdued, sedate pitch.

Those changes were nothing more than a bunch of superficial stuff, Flynn knew. But how else could he show Molly that he was serious, responsible, trustable? And it was starting to panic him that it didn't seem to be working. Nothing seemed to be working. In the past few days, Molly...

The phone jangled on his desk just as he walked in, interrupting that whole thought train—not that this day hadn't been a nonstop mess of interruptions anyway. He plunked Dylan down and impatiently grabbed the receiver.

"Flynn? This is Virginie."

His tongue suddenly felt like sandpaper. He sank into his office chair. For weeks now, every single time the phone rang, he'd expected the caller to be her. "I can't believe you didn't call before this. You realize you never left me an address, a phone, any way to reach you—"

Her voice had started out quiet but immediately turned defensive. "I told you that I didn't know where I'd be—that I'd lost my job, had to find another place to live. Everything in my life was a mess. But I had to call. I just wanted to know if Dylan's all right."

"Dylan's fine. Full of hell." At the moment the baby was pulling paper out of his spewing fax, and bunching it up in exuberant fists. Flynn considered stopping him, but hell. If the president of the free world were sending that fax, it was too late to recover it now anyway.

"I told you he was trouble. Other babies sleep. He doesn't. He could wear our ten adults without half trying. I couldn't handle it. Maybe now you understand. Did you have the blood test?"

"Yes, I had the test." He'd also complained about the baby himself, using practically the same words. But it sounded so different, coming from her. He'd always meant humor, where Virginie sounded dead serious.

"I didn't think there was much point in calling until you'd had time to get the tests and results back. So you can't pretend he's not your responsibility, Flynn. And it won't kill you to know what it's like. All the work, all the messes, all the worrying. You can't have any kind of life with a baby around. You never get a moment to yourself."

Flynn squeezed his eyes closed. Listening to her made memories snipe his mind like bullets. He remembered the scotch haze of that party. Remembered that she was pretty—a sexy type of pretty, not Molly's far more lethally natural type of sexiness. There was no comparing a rhinestone to a diamond, but Flynn's conscience was too merciless to pretend that Virginie hadn't attracted him then. Or that he'd never noticed her shallowness. What bit sharpest, though, was the measure of his own shallowness in choosing that kind of woman to be with.

Baby claws hooked on his pants leg, distracting him. Dylan. Pulling himself up, then letting go to stand free, his fat diapered fanny wagging like a sail in an uncertain breeze. Before he could crash—and cry—Flynn reached out a hand to steady him.

"Virginie, is that the only reason you called?" he asked carefully. "To ask if the baby was okay?"

"Yeah. Basically." She hesitated. "I found a job, a new apartment. And I met someone. He's on his way up, been good to me so far. But babies…he doesn't want to be tied down with babies."

His heart felt a strange clutching. For weeks he'd assumed she'd call. But for weeks he assumed her reason for calling would be to demand the kid back. God knew, the advent of the baby had thrown issues of pride, honor and respect right in his face. It was the damn baby that altered Molly's whole opinion of him. It was the damn baby that forced him to look in the mirror—and figure out he didn't like what he saw there.

Only somehow, mysteriously, he'd come to love the damn baby more than life. He'd started out scared about being a decent father. After weeks with Dylan, that was sure no better, more like ten times worse—he was more petrified instead of less. It didn't seem to matter. Dylan was his *son,* part of the beat and pulse of his heart. And he felt stricken with dread at even the thought of Virginie threatening to take him away. "That's really the only reason you called? Not to make arrangements to see him?"

"Obviously you haven't been listening. I'm not even in the same state. I can't just pop over there to visit him. And if you're trying to lay some guilt trip on me—"

"I'm not," he said swiftly. Dylan had bent his head and spotted all the electrical connections for the computer set up under his desk. Flynn had seen that love-of-danger gleam in his eyes before.

Swiftly he scooped the baby onto his lap, at the same time telling himself to think. Hard. Fast. Carefully. "I'm not criticizing you for anything. You did what you felt you had to do. But at some point, things need to be more…settled. For the sake of the baby's security. There are choices, including all kinds of legal custody arrangements—I don't know what you might be willing to consider—"

He heard a short, humorous laugh. "I don't have to legally do anything to have rights, Flynn. I'm the mother. It works for me the way it is right now—all your problem. And you're the one with the ton of money. You take care of his security."

"At least leave me a phone number where I can contact you—"

But abruptly he heard a dial tone. She'd hung up on him…just as the baby reached over his arm, punched a keyboard button and made three hours of work disappear from the computer screen.

Flynn grabbed the baby and lifted him high in the air, making Dylan giggle and blow bubbles. "You think I want you?" he muttered. "You think I'd fight to the death for you? You're a monster. A royal, bubble-blowing total pain in the keister."

Dylan pumped his legs, thrilled with this whole

game…and then Bailey showed up in the doorway. "Hey, you're late for the staff meeting."

"I'm coming." But as he lurched out of the chair, carrying twenty pounds of trouble under his arm, his throat went as dry as sandpaper again.

His life seemed to be as out of control as a typhoon. He had a baby he didn't know how to father. A business that was temporarily running ten miles faster than him. No answers for how to handle a woman in his past who seemed so damned selfish he was ashamed to know her.

And he was in love. With Molly. Like he'd never been in love, or like he'd believed love could be part of his life. She wasn't the only critical problem on his plate, but she was the thread running between them all. She'd ransomed his heart. Earning her respect had somehow become inexorably linked with earning his own self-respect back. He wasn't just trying to change his life for her— but for both of them. Because to lose Molly, Flynn feared, was to lose his chance to become the man he could be, wanted to be.

Molly was just digging into her coat pocket for gloves when she rounded the corner near Flynn's office—and heard Gretchen's voice. It was almost six, and most of the staff cleared out around five. Gretchen was standing in Flynn's doorway, wearing a jean jacket as if she were on the verge of leaving for the day, too. Molly wouldn't have thought anything of it if she hadn't caught the girl's raised voice.

"I'm sorry, Mr. McGannon, but I mean it. I'm quitting."

"Gretchen, I can see you're unhappy, but I honestly don't understand what the problem is—"

"*You're* the problem. You won't let me do my job.

This is crazy. I can't just sit around and do nothing. Every time I start doing something with the baby, you come in and take him!''

''Now, I don't do that all the time—''

''Yeah, you do.'' Big sniffs. ''I say no, you say yes. Every time he lets out a little cry, you're standing in the doorway, looking at me like I'm an ax murderer. Nobody can stop a baby from crying every time, Mr. McGannon, they're *babies*, for Pete's sake. I don't know what you hired me for. You never let me do anything.''

''Holy kamoly. Don't cry, okay? Please. Hell, I didn't mean to do anything to make you upset. If we talk about this—''

''I *did* talk to you. Three times now. You don't listen. You don't trust anybody with that baby but you. I've had it. I mean it. I'm quitting. You just send my last paycheck.''

Molly watched the girl spin around, jam a stocking cap onto her head, and march for the front doors. Once that door closed, the only sound in the whole place was the hum of fluorescent lights.

Molly hesitated, then edged forward and peered around the doorway. Flynn was sprawled in his office chair as if he'd just thrown himself there, his expression baffled. Even if she hadn't made a sound, he spotted her faster than radar.

''Did you just see Gretchen?''

''Yes.''

''Mol—she quit. Just now. Just like that.''

''I heard.''

''She started crying. Hell. I feel like sh…I feel awful. I know I'm not too cool in the tact and sensitivity department, but I swear I didn't do anything to deliberately hurt her feelings.''

"Nothing you said necessarily made her cry, Flynn. She was upset. She lost control." Molly stepped in. She could see Dylan indulging in a late nap, curled up in his hammock, but the rest of Flynn's office looked like an alien had taken up residence here. Baby toys littered the place, but Dylan's debris reproduced everywhere in the building. Flynn's "toys" were gone, cupboards and drawers closed, his desk heaped with work—but in immaculately organized files. It wasn't natural. It wasn't normal.

And Flynn himself looked like an alien clone of the Real McGannon. His blue oxford shirt was starched, for Pete's sake. His dark slacks were neatly creased. He was wearing shoes—in the office yet—and a recent haircut made him look like some darn fool executive. But the worst, and most noticeable, change in his appearance was the no-smile.

She hadn't heard Flynn's roar of laughter in ages, hadn't heard him yell at anyone on the staff. He was talking in pleases and thank-yous. He'd quit telling wicked off-color jokes, hadn't expressed a single wild-eyed boisterous idea, and was walking around like the sedate CEO he was supposed to be. The whole staff was worried he was having a nervous breakdown.

So was Molly. None of these personality changes had been instant; they'd been evolving over the past two weeks. He was trying so hard. She had absolutely no idea what he was doing, but he seemed to be half killing himself trying to do it—and it was getting tough not to notice that this drastic metamorphosis had begun after the night they'd made love.

Not that Molly had ever thought of herself as a Cleopatra under the sheets—but for a man to turn from an exuberant life-lover into an aspiring funeral director after making love to her tended to be crippling on her feminine ego.

"Mol..." He swung out of his office chair, his mind obviously still focused on his now-defunct baby-sitter. "I don't even get why she quit, why she was so upset."

Her heart did that slow melt thing and all he was doing was pacing in front of her. "Um, McGannon...do you think there's just a slim chance you might be a teensy bit overprotective of the baby?"

Those bushy eyebrows shot up in shock. "How can anybody possibly be too overprotective with a baby? You can't gamble on a kid's safety, Mol."

"I agree. Completely. But—" She struggled to find words when all she really wanted to do was hug him. He looked so...alone. But this new grave-as-a-judge Flynn hadn't invited any touches, hadn't flirted, hadn't pounced on her in over a week now. It would seem obvious he wanted some distance, except that he went miles out of his way to seek time with her. He was sending so many mixed signals that she felt confounded what to do, what to think.

"You trust the baby with me," she pointed out.

"Well, yeah, of course. But you're you. Gretchen—or any other baby-sitter—is the same as a stranger."

"She's a stranger who had a ton more experience with babies than the two of us put together." But she was wasting her breath, she thought. The whole staff had seen him charge upstairs every time Dylan let out a whimper. No one was going to be surprised in the morning that Gretchen quit. But getting Flynn to even consider lightening up about the baby at the moment, Molly suspected, had as much chance of getting through to bedrock. He looked too stressed, too beat. And the baby was stirring.

"Something tells me you had a challenging day even before the problem with Gretchen?"

"Yeah. This whole day's been a nonstop pressure cooker. Including a call from Virginie…" He dragged a hand through his hair and abruptly frowned. "You brought me a bunch of stuff this morning I was supposed to look at, didn't you?"

"Yes, the end-of-the-month accounts. And the new projects coming in—I can't even get those on the books until we've sat down together. I need a couple of hours with you, Flynn."

"Yeah, I know. I just haven't gotten to it yet. But I'll start on it right now, if you want…what're you doing?"

"Getting your coat. And looking for Dylan's coat. He's up—I'm guessing he'll need a diaper change—and then I'm taking you guys to dinner." Her voice was firm. More work was the last thing Flynn needed. With no baby-sitter, projects piled half to the ceiling, and a man looking hollow-eyed from lack of sleep…well, it was perfectly obvious someone had to take charge.

"Molly, there's no place we could take Dylan to dinner."

"Sure there is."

"Restaurants have health codes. Probably most neighborhoods have noise ordinances, too. You've seen Dylan eat—"

"Uh-huh. And I know just the place. Don't waste your breath arguing with me, McGannon, you'll just lose. You're hungry. So am I. So's the baby. You're going to need a work plan if you're without a baby-sitter again. Nobody, but nobody, can organize someone else's life as well as I can."

There, she thought. Finally a grin from him. Being nice

to the man had never worked. Boss him around like a shrew and McGannon always came around.

She grinned back at him, but there was no way to put wattage in the smile. A leaden feeling of dread was chugging through her pulse. She started moving, fast, so he wouldn't realize how upset she was. Once the baby's diaper was changed, coats on and the office locked up, she hustled the two of them out to the parking lot.

Snowflakes were drifting down, as fragile as moonbeams, softer than stars. Like the shape her heart was in, she thought. She'd heard him mention the call from Virginie, and couldn't help but notice how swiftly he'd dropped the subject. From the day Dylan appeared in his life, Flynn had only willingly turned to one person for help. Her. Molly had seen that as a positive measure that he uniquely trusted her, but she'd always feared that need in his life was temporary. Flynn was a strong, tough cookie—once he figured out how deeply he loved his son, her fulfilling a need in that equation simply disappeared. His behavior these past couple of weeks, and now, his dropping something so important to him as that call from Virginie, seemed painfully obvious clues that he was pushing her away.

She was losing this man of her heart. And temporarily she just didn't know what to do—except try to shake that vulnerable, crushing fear. Her two guys needed care and feeding. At least that job was something she knew how to do.

Flynn drove—because his Cherokee had the baby's car seat—but Molly motioned where she wanted him to pull in. He chuckled when he saw the golden arches. "Well, if there's a place in the universe this could work, it has to be here," he admitted.

A few minutes later, everything seemed better to Molly.

Once Flynn started loosening up and relaxing, she found she could, too. The place really was exactly what the doctor ordered. There were lots of teenagers wolfing down Big Macs, but just as many harried-looking young parents, toting kids too young to behave in a sit-down restaurant.

Their pride and joy seemed to be the homeliest—and loudest—baby in the place. Personally Molly thought the others lacked even half of Dylan's character and spirit, but possibly love colored her judgment. It was a little late to pretend she hadn't fallen as hard and irrevocably for the squirt as she had for the squirt's dad.

The squirt's dad inhaled dinner as if he hadn't eaten in a week. Molly took over the devil, feeding baby food and formula from the stash in the diaper bag. Predictably Dylan finished that and immediately wanted what they were having. Flynn spent a good five minutes lecturing his son about how nutrition and dietary habits could affect his whole life, possibly his IQ, how studies about junk food had shown it negatively affected performance on tests and could even affect whether he got into the right college...at least until Molly cracked up.

"That's it, McGannon, I'm gonna take all those parenting books away from you and burn them. One single French fry cannot possibly change the child's entire destiny. Now either you give him one or I will."

"You think I'm a little overserious on this parenting business?"

"Does the word 'rabid' mean anything to you?"

Flynn promptly gave his son a French fry—one—but his eyes were on her. "Well, if it took being a little rabid, it got you laughing, didn't it?"

Well, yeah, it had, making Molly conscious that Flynn had picked up on her earlier troubled mood, too. But they both had to chuckle at Dylan's response to the single French fry. He loved it. Beyond loved it.

The phrase "good as gold" rarely applied to their darling, but they actually finished the meal in peace. Unfortunately the fast food restaurant had a playground built inside. Every kid under ten was whooping it up, charging around the jungle gyms and slides. Dylan started bouncing and making urgent hand motions. It wasn't hard to interpret that he wanted to be playing with the other children.

"You're too little," Flynn told him. "Those are big kids out there. You'd get creamed. Once you master the walking thing a little better, we'll talk about it again."

For the first time since they'd walked in, Dylan let out a wailing bellow. Loud enough to turn heads. Flynn sighed. "Am I gonna let him win?" he asked Molly.

"As if there was any question. If you want to just sit still and relax for a while, I'll carry him around in there."

But they both went in together, neither realizing that behind the noise-buffering glass doors, there was bedlam. Children raced every which way, amid screams and shrieks. It was Dylan's natural milieu. Flynn, holding him securely, whooshed him down the slide and fake-walked him up a play ladder.

Startling her completely, he brought up Virginie's call—and relayed the whole gist of the conversation in the middle of all the mayhem. If he was willing to talk about it—here or anywhere else—Molly wasn't about to let it go.

"So what did you think? After she hung up like that?"

Flynn crouched down and pushed Dylan in a little tire swing, keeping one hand on him the whole time. "The truth? I thought I wished to hell I'd never laid eyes on her. And then I wish that you never had to know I was ever involved with a woman like that." Blue eyes blazed on hers with raw emotion—but only for a second. Dylan took two eyes—and four pairs of hands—to keep safe in this environment.

Molly righted a pint-size imp who barreled into her legs. "If you were never involved with her, you'd never have your son, Flynn."

"Yeah. It took me a while, but I came to that conclusion, too. And this has to sound funny coming from me. You know I never felt sure about this fathering business. But somebody has to love him. Really love him. And give a serious damn about his whole future."

She almost held her breath. It was a running joke in the office how inseparably Flynn had bonded to the baby. McGannon seemed the only one who hadn't noticed he was crazy about his son—but then he'd always been as blind as a bat about himself. "I have to believe she'll call again. That she'll change her mind about wanting to see Dylan at some point."

"I do, too. I can't believe she's as cold-blooded as she comes across. Right now I just think she likes it. She likes believing she's put me in this limbo—legalwise and life-wise, too. I've got the baby, but only until she changes her mind."

That's exactly what Molly was afraid of…and was just as afraid of for Flynn. "Have you thought about going to court? Applying for a specific custody arrangement, with you as the primary guardian?"

"Yeah, I've thought about it. But I'm not sure pushing Virginie is a good idea. Both times she's contacted me now, she's made a big point out of not leaving me a phone number or address. Silly, really. With a name and social security number, it's not hard to track down anyone. I could find her. But she's made it clear as crystal that she

doesn't want to deal with this right now.'' Dylan tired of
the swing and motioned to the slide again.

Flynn carted him back there, letting dozens of little
bodies jostle past him. ''Forcing her hand could be a gamble. And I don't want to gamble—anything—affecting
Dylan. My lawyer told me that her deserting the baby is
a major card against her, but that isn't the whole poker
game. Courts almost always find for the natural mother.
She could claim temporary financial circumstances were
the only motivating factor in that desertion. And I'm not
kidding myself—I don't look like anybody's hero in that
picture, for getting her pregnant, and then for not being
part of the baby's life until all this time later. Bottom
line—if I push her, tick her off by going through the court
system—I could lose. Not lose rights to see him. But
rights to be his primary guardian. Um, Molly…''

She had to smile. ''Yeah, I see you have your hands
full. We can finish talking about this later.'' Everything
he'd said, everything he'd been grappling with—alone—
wrenched her heart and had her mind spinning thoughts
and reactions.

Just then, though, Dylan had him full-scale busy. The
baby was laughing with big, bubbly, delighted belly
laughs. Flynn, holding him tight, whooshed him down the
slide and then whirled him in the air sky-high several
times. Eventually, though, the baby seemed to figure out
that all the big kids were getting to the top of the slide a
different way. The slide was constructed with a round
plastic cubicle at the top—all the other children were
emerging from that round circle. Dylan started making
hand motions that he wanted to climb and go down the
way they were.

Molly couldn't help but chuckle, feeling charmed. Dad
and son weren't making a lick of sense, to anyone but

each other. Flynn was arguing in grown-up English. Dylan was arguing back in squalls and gestures and *"babloobs"* and *"damoos."* Yet the two of them seemed to think they understood each other perfectly.

"Cripes, Dyl, you do love danger. I'm telling you straight. You're not going up there without me, and I'm not sure the equipment's strong enough to hold my weight."

Her chuckle promptly died. "McGannon, you can't go up there. It's for pipsqueak-size people only. There's a sign—"

"I know. But he really wants to go to the top of the slide. And he's having such a great time…" Flynn, squint-eyed, studied the construction, and started handling some of the base structure to determine its sturdiness.

"Flynn! You won't fit in that circular hole at the top!" A couple of small children got into the discussion, all urging Flynn to go for it with the baby. Molly's jaw dropped. The darn fool had already taken the mini-ladder steps up and disappeared under a plastic crawl space.

Seconds later, Dylan's body emerged—Flynn's hands around his waist, the baby waving his hands in uproarious excitement, chanting, "Da! Da! Da!"

"You ready to catch him at the bottom, Mol?"

Of course she was ready to catch him. And between Flynn's long arms and hers, the baby wasn't on his own for even a second on the slide ride. Molly lifted Dylan in the air with a 'whoosh' the way Flynn had, but then unfortunately turned her head.

McGannon's arms and shoulders and head were sticking out of the circular hole. Only he couldn't seem to back up. And he was positively too big to go down. "Uh…Mol? I seem to be in a little dilemma here. I think it's what they call a tight squeeze."

"Do we know him?" She asked Dylan. "I'm certainly not willing to admit I know him at the moment. How about if we go back in and get you another French fry..."

"Mol! Mol! You can't leave me here!"

Eleven

Flynn threaded the baby into the car seat, strapped him in and then straightened up. Molly was right there, waiting to climb into the back seat next to Dylan—assuming she got control of herself sometime in the next millennium. Tears of laughter were no longer sputtering from her eyes, but the parking lot's neon lights brilliantly illuminated her sick attempt at a deadpan expression.

"Good thing McDonalds have a lot of franchises, huh? Because somehow I don't think you'll be in a hustle to come back to this one."

"Hey, the manager understood. He said I wasn't the only parent who'd had a slight...mishap...on the playground trying to help his kid."

"I believe what the manager said, McGannon, was that an incredible number of adults ignore the signs all over the place prohibiting big people from getting on the equipment." Molly delicately coughed. The cough was an effort to stop herself from giggling. It hadn't worked before and it didn't now. The cough turned into a gloating chuckle, which eventually turned into a full-fledged belly laugh. Again. "Oh, God. Oh, God. I can hardly wait to get to work tomorrow—"

"Now, Mol, let's not do anything hasty. There's no reason the staff has to hear anything about this—"

"They do! They do! They need to know."

He hammed up an exaggerated, exhausted sigh. "Okay. I admit I'm vulnerable to some blackmail. What's it gonna take for you to keep quiet about this?"

"Trust me, you don't have enough money, Flynn. I can just see Bailey's face when I tell this story. And Simone's—"

The problem, Flynn mused, was that he could see *her* face.

All lit up with laughter. Eyes dancing, cheeks flushed, lips parted. She hadn't had this much fun teasing him in weeks—and for damn sure she hadn't been this no-nerves, easy-with-him relaxed. Hell, it was almost enough to inspire him into climbing that darn kid's slide and getting stuck all over again.

"—And Ralph's. And Darren's—"

"Does the word 'mercy' mean nothing to you, Weston?"

"In your dreams. Gee, I wonder if they have security cameras. Maybe I can get a videotape of you squished at the top of the slide, all those little kids trying to help you, peddle it to CNN for the national news—"

Well, that did it. She was still muttering inglorious plans as she brushed past him to climb into the back seat. A simple tug on her wrist made her head shoot up. Her eyes blinked wide in surprise—for the whole second it took to level her against the side of the Cherokee.

She was asking for trouble. He knew it. She knew it. Anyone looking at that sassy teasing-a-man-beyond-reason smile would know it, but damn. He'd successfully kept his hands off her. Nothing about the relationship could work unless he proved that respect business. There was a whole list of stuff he was trying to show her—self-control, responsibility, seriousness, maturity, ethics, all that junk that mattered to Mol. Hell, it mattered to him. And he'd sworn to leave her alone until he'd proved to her that the guy she was ashamed of had changed.

Some change. Acting like a darn fool kid and humiliatingly getting himself stuck on a child's slide was the exact opposite of every goal in his head, his heart, his soul. At the time, it had just been an impulse. In the spirit of fun and keeping Dylan happy. A tiny gamble with principles of physics that he'd sure as hell lost.

He knew better than to gamble, and he knew better than to kiss her. Everything was wrong.

Until he touched her. And then nothing in his entire life seemed as right as this. The instant his lips touched down, her arms slowly lifted to rope around his neck. She met his mouth, met his kiss, as if she'd been waiting, waiting, waiting for the perfect opportunity to drive him stark crazy.

No one tasted like her. Sweet, supple, yielding soft. Desire stirred like a torrent and torment both. The baby was yawning in his car seat, snuggled two blankets thick, oblivious to the chaos being generated right next to him. A car backfired. Neon lights glared. Strangers walked by. Yet she kissed him back with winsome abandon, her breasts gloved against his chest, her pelvis rocking against his with provocative intimacy. How such a wholesome woman could cause such devilment, he neither knew nor cared. Molly could turn into pure fire, when she wanted.

She could make an iceberg melt, when she wanted. She could make a man believe he was everything that ever mattered to her.

Reluctantly he surfaced for air. So did she. Her eyelashes fluttered up. Her eyes, as black as midnight, rested softly on his face. "You think you're bribing my silence, McGannon?" she whispered.

"Hell, no. I don't care if you tell the whole damn world anything you want."

"You haven't kissed me in days."

"Not because I didn't want to. I was trying..." He hesitated. "Damn, have I been an insensitive jerk again?" You thought I didn't want you?" She didn't answer, but he saw her eyes. *"No,"* he said gruffly. "I've been going crazy, thinking about you, wanting you. Trying to stay away from you. I just..."

"You just what, Flynn?"

But he felt as trapped as a rat in a maze. There was no explaining that he wanted her respect, because the words alone meant nothing—he'd either earned it or he'd failed to. And he'd never been one of those New Age guys who easily talked about emotional stuff, but he tried. "We kind of tumbled into bed. I was afraid you'd regret it. I didn't want you unhappy about making love with me, being involved with me. I wanted to prove something to you."

She touched his cheek, her expression sober now. "What is this thing you wanted to prove?"

"That you could trust me."

Her delicate eyebrows arched like wings. "You trying to insult me, McGannon? I'd never have made love with you if I didn't trust you. You think I'm a dimwit?"

"No. Good grief, no. I didn't mean anything like that..." He clawed a hand through his hair. "Look, trying to talk about this in a public parking lot is crazy. And I need to put the monster to bed.'' His eyes searched hers. ''Come home with me?''

She hesitated. ''Okay.''

Her car was still in the office parking lot, but Flynn suspected that worrying about transportation logistics had nothing to do with her hesitation. She didn't need to worry—about anything. They weren't going to follow through with that inflammatory kiss. They were going to talk. Seriously talk.

Driving home and putting the baby to bed gave him ample time to put his mental house in order. He never had been sure why Molly slept with him, but he needed to make certain things were right with her. No matter what else she thought of him, he needed her to believe that he seriously cared about her. He'd never been looking for a fast, selfish lay with the ante of her emotions at stake.

He had all the words planned out in his head. Only it took several minutes to diaper and bottle and rock Dylan. And by the time he walked back downstairs...well, it seemed Molly had used that time. She'd slipped off her shoes, turned off the lights, started a whistling-little fire in the hearth. The yellow flames caught the glow of two wineglasses.

One glance at the scene made his pulse pick up an edgy beat. One glance at her had his pulse accelerate that beat to a rush. She'd neatly folded her suit jacket on a chair, and was sitting on the white rug with her legs drawn up. The silky ivory blouse looked as soft as her skin. The slim skirt outlined her hips and led down to long, slim, stockinged legs. He could smell wood smoke and her perfume.

He could smell his dead-serious intentions scattering like seeds in a wind. Hormones charged through his bloodstream faster than a jet on takeoff. Dammit, he just couldn't let that happen.

Her face lifted to his in a warm smile of greeting. "You get slugger to sleep okay?"

"Yeah, he's out for the count. Molly, we need to talk," he said firmly.

She nodded, patting the space on the rug next to her. "I know we do. I've been worried about you, McGannon."

"Worried?"

"Uh-huh. You've been a disaster for the past few days—long face, no smile, sober as a judge. Until I heard you laugh tonight—really laugh—I was starting to worry you must be sick. Now obviously something is really bothering you, and I can't read your mind. C'mere. Kick off your shoes, have a sip of wine and start talking."

He pushed off his shoes, plunked down cross-legged, and kicked back a slug of wine. If Molly thought it took an illness for him to behave in a sober, serious, responsible way, this conversation had nowhere to go but up. Hell, all week he'd been trying to impress her with his model good guy behavior. That had obviously bombed. He didn't have much choice but to try being his normal blunt, blundering self. "Yeah. There was something bothering me. Still is. I've been afraid of hurting you."

She stared at him thoughtfully for a moment, and then her voice turned velvet-soft. "Because we made love?"

"Yeah. In part. Mol...how many times have you slept with a guy where you didn't think the relationship was headed for a commitment, marriage?"

"Never," she admitted.

"Uh-huh. Then along comes this guy who can't keep his hands off you. And the chemistry between them could power a continent or two. I didn't back off because I didn't want to make love with you. But because I did. And I didn't want you to feel pressured or pushed into pursuing something that may not be right for you.''

"You've never pressured me in any way, Flynn. You stole some kisses...but you also backed off anytime I hinted at a no.'' Her firelit profile made her hair look like spun silk, her eyes lush-soft. ''You think hormones is the only reason I got involved with you?''

"I don't know. But I know from your shoes, I have to look a hell of a bad gamble.''

Something sparked in her eyes that made him feel...rattled. But her voice was still that butter-smooth gentle tone. ''You don't think I could love you, Mc-Gannon?''

"I think when we were messing around, flirting, it wasn't hurting you. You weren't risking anything that was going to cost you. You were so shy, Mol, so tucked into yourself. Watching you flirt back, kiss back, start to swing those hips when you walked—''

"I *never* did that.''

For the first time he had to grin, even if it didn't last. ''Oh, yeah, you did. And yeah, you do. And I loved watching you come into your own. Loved watching that natural confidence and sass come to life. Only...'' He took a breath. ''Only it was always really important to me—not to hurt someone else, to make them pay for my mistakes. My dad—he always had someone or something to blame but himself, and he always took the people down around him.''

"And you think you're like that?''

"I hope to God I'm not. But it has to look that way from your shoes. You and I tangled closer at the worst possible time. You know I had a fly-by-night affair with Virginie. You've seen me floundering with the baby. You kept getting dragged into helping me...but damned if I can see what you thought I had to offer you."

"McGannon, you're being awfully hard on yourself."

"I'm trying to be honest with you."

"Fine. Then I'll be honest right back. You've got a heart bigger than the sky. An imagination that just doesn't fit into neat little boundaries. You opened my life by just watching—your courage, your spirit, your laughter, your willingness to always open the door to the possibilities. You squeeze every ounce of life out of every day. And you're beyond an incredible lover because you love that way, too."

"Um, Mol..."

"I'm talking. Don't interrupt, buster."

But she wasn't talking. She scooched closer and then she pushed him in the chest, and when he was leveled on the scratchy white rug, she vented a kiss full of fury and lightning.

He saw her scooching. He anticipated her smooching. He could have stopped her. There were still things that needed saying. Flynn was unsure if he had the right to bring up a future and rings, felt even less sure if Molly wanted to hear those words from him. But what mattered now, immediately, was her believing he loved her. He didn't want Mol looking back on anything she'd done with him and feeling shame.

But shame really didn't seem to be a problem at this precise moment. Kissing her back was a consuming occupation. It was impossible not to revel in the woman in his arms. The phrase hell-bent-for-leather came to mind, then that lush, soft mouth of hers obliterated any prayer of his trying to think. There were nails on those fingers of hers, clawing at his shirt.

A long, slim leg insinuated itself between his thighs

and evocatively rubbed against him. The crackle and hiss of fire had nothing on the heat she was inspiring. When her head reared up, her eyes had that fierce fire glow.

"I'll love you if I damn well want to, Flynn."

It'd take a gutsier man than him to argue with her.

"You made some mistakes. But you're so damned blind I think that's all you see. I don't love jerks. You hear me?"

"Yes, Mol."

"I sure as hell wouldn't be taking off my blouse if you were a jerk."

"Yes, Mol."

"Get rid of that shirt."

"Yes, Mol."

"You are so *frustrating*. Thinking you know how my shoes fit. Deciding I was going to be hurt. Not asking *me*. You think I'm not smart enough to figure out what I want and need in my own life?"

"God. No, Mol—"

"Well, you can just shut up, McGannon. You're all through talking. You're real good at tearing yourself down. But now it's my turn to get a word in."

As far as he noticed, he wasn't doing any talking. And as soon as she claimed she was, she quit. Her blouse was draping the edge of the coffee table by then. He was stark naked except for one sock—and the wallet he'd plucked from his pants pocket before all hell broke loose. He hadn't retrieved the protection from it yet, but one crisis at a time. He only had two hands and both were busy.

She leveled him with another kiss, deep and dark enough to make him think of wild oceans with no life buoy in sight. Her tongue dipped into his mouth, dragged against his. For something so small and wet and soft, that tongue speared razor-sharp need all through him.

He twisted her around so she was on top, better to protect her soft skin from the scruffy-textured rug. Maybe that saved her skin, but it sacrificed his sanity. His ever-logical, relentlessly thorough CPA was meticulously auditing his body parts. She tucked her legs around him, her pelvis shimmying against his, her fingertips whispering over throat, chest, exploring ribs and muscle, accounting for his manic heartbeat. Her bare breasts, scooped in his hands, looked like ivory in the firelight...wet ivory, when he leaned up to lave her taut nipples with his tongue.

One hand blind-slapped the rug, slapped the hearth, slapped around until his fist closed on his wallet. He thought of his redheaded Dylan before he yanked out a condom, thought that Dylan just might not mind a honey-haired angel of a sister...thought of a time when fatherhood had seemed alien to anything he could have in life. But those wild blurry thoughts were abruptly shelved for another time. He would not risk Molly, not have her ever believing again that he'd do something irresponsible that could risk her.

Oh, those eyes of hers. They shuttered closed, lashes laying on her cheeks like soot on snow, as he slowly eased her onto him. She was hot, wet, warm, encasing him inch by inch, and when she was seated for the ride to come, intimately and inseparably part of him, she opened her eyes again.

He saw the wicked feminine smile. And he saw pride, in her face, in her touch, pride in her femininity and sexuality that she offered him like a gift.

But it was the love in her eyes that took him under. She loved him. Impossible not to believe, when that love was like a light bursting inside her...love that washed over him and filled him from the inside out. There was a time he'd been afraid of letting anyone this close. In the back of his heart, he was still afraid he hadn't earned that rich, lush freely offered love from Molly.

Just then, though, her heartbeat seemed inseparable from his. He wanted her like a tearing need, like a shard of his soul belonged to her and nothing existed but her and him and this joyful ride straight to oblivion. She cried out something willful and wild. Not enough. He wanted more for her, drove her higher, hotter, until a second climax rippled through her whole body and explosively triggered his own.

It took a while before he could catch his breath. Gradually he became aware of the fire's snap and hiss, the soft yellow shadows dancing on the walls, but he didn't move. Didn't want to. Molly's weight felt perfect, her warmth and softness invoking an intimate, treasuring feeling of belonging. He stroked her hair, the silken strands catching the firelight, his eyes half-closed...until he heard her soft-voiced lazy whisper.

"Well, I guess I showed you, huh?"

He had to grin. They were just such big words for a lady who was collapsed like a dishrag on his chest. "Um, is there anything in particular you were trying to show me? Beyond an alternative view of the universe? And what an incredible, breathtakingly beautiful woman you are?"

She chuckled, but she didn't lift her head from its nesting spot on his shoulder. "I was just thinking those incredible and beautiful words about you, too...but I had in mind something a little more serious. Did you happen to notice that something pretty darn spectacular happened between us?"

"Offhand, I'd say spectacular doesn't begin to describe it, but...yeah. I more than noticed."

She nuzzled her cheek closer. "After we made love the

first time, you turned off a light switch. You're never gonna pull that nonsense again, are you? Because that was pretty darn scary on my feminine ego.''

His arms tightened instinctively around her. "Mol...I swear that was my last intent on earth. I never meant to hurt you."

"I know you didn't. Just don't cut me off again, okay? You had a problem that was really troubling you. I understand that, and I understand that you're not used to someone in your life that you can depend on. But...we showed each other just what we could do, yes? If those doors are just open? So talk to me if there's something on your mind."

"Okay. There's something on my mind. I need you to know something."

"Yeah?"

"I love you, Molly Weston."

Her head lifted then. Eyes softer than rainbows rested on his face. "You mean it this time, don't you?" she whispered. "Not just lip service."

"I mean it from the heart. I. Really. Love. You."

There was a moment's silence. And then Molly scooched up a little higher, found his mouth and launched a second full-scale love assault that lasted long into the night.

Flynn kept thinking: this can't be real. He kept thinking: but it was. She was. Right then he couldn't imagine anything more perfect than Molly in his arms and his life. And for the first time he believed he had a chance with her, a real chance at a future, if he just didn't screw up.

Twelve

Things were darn near perfect, Molly mused. She carried her coffee mug to the glass doors in the break room, sipping as she looked out. This close to Thanksgiving, the winter sun lazed in until almost nine in the morning. It was just peaking over the horizon now, the air as sharp as crystal, and a ground cover of snow looked like whipped cream with a pale pink glaze.

Behind her, Bailey growled a greeting as he got his first mug of coffee, disappeared, and then Ralph bebopped in with a "Yo, Mol" before mainlining his favorite brew. The staff meeting was scheduled in a few minutes, but she was already well prepared for that. She had time to savor the magical dawn for a few more moments, time to reflect how her whole life felt magical these days…except for a ring on her finger. But Molly quickly pushed away that thought.

Flynn had changed so much in the past few weeks.

She'd been over to his place almost every night. After Gretchen quit, he'd really been snowed under. A new caregiver had been hired—Mrs. Hanson. Molly had helped him with that, helped him brainstorm ways to rearrange his life and work to accommodate the time he wanted with the baby. But they'd made love darn near incessantly.

And talked almost as much. Molly no longer feared she was another Virginie in his life. The love was there, real, visible in the way he treated her, touched her, looked at her. If she felt uneasy to have her toothpaste installed in his bathroom without a ring, that was just dumb, she'd told herself. Archaic puritan values. Of course she'd always been tediously puritanical, but with Flynn's background, it was a slow road, learning to trust and open up. He was trying…and their times together had been as magical as this special morning.

Bailey stomped in behind her, wearing his lucky bathrobe over a blue checked shirt. "Hey, Molly, it's almost nine. You know where Flynn is?"

She glanced at the clock, then splashed some fresh coffee into her mug. "He said he was going to get in a couple of hours' work in at home—assuming the baby'd accommodate him by sleeping in. We can start without him if he's not here. But if you need something specific, maybe you should shoot a call to his house?"

"I did that. But there was no answer."

"Then he's probably on his way here." Molly grabbed her files and mug and headed for Brainstorming Central. Simone was already installed in an easy chair, in a long flowing caftan that matched her turban.

"It seems everyone's moving slow this morning except for us," Simone commented. "Flynn isn't here?"

"Not yet."

"Is that new baby-sitter looking like she's going to work out?"

"Mrs. Hanson? Yeah, so far." Molly started arranging work, guessing she was going to be stuck starting the meeting. "She only wants part-time work, but she's real flexible on the schedule...she's also a grandma type. Flynn's listening to her—now there's a miracle—and she's already got him and Dylan ten times more organized at the house than they were before."

Simone chuckled. "He's pretty hopeless with that baby. Bailey said something about the mother calling again?"

Molly settled in a chair with a leg tucked under her. Flynn never ducked a question about his private life with the staff, so neither had she. For him, the staff was almost family. "Virginie. Yes. She's thinking about marrying some guy and changed her mind about Dylan and custody. Now she wants it on paper that Flynn is responsible—legally, financially, the whole shot. Made out like she'd sue him if he didn't go along, which is almost funny, considering it's exactly what he wanted. At some point, we both think she's going to change her mind and want to see Dyl. But right now securing his future is the main thing."

"And what about your future in that picture, Molly?" Simone wrapped long elegant fingers around her coffee mug.

"My future?"

"You're in love with him," Simone said quietly.

"Yeah. I am." Molly could no more have denied the sun rising in the morning, but she felt surprised and a little touched at the direction of the conversation. Simone had always been ultrareserved until the past few weeks.

"And the whole place knows he's beside himself in love with you. He can't take his eyes off you. But..."

Simone regarded her over the rim of her coffee cup. "All men are animals, girl, and don't you believe otherwise. They'd stay wild forever if they had a choice. Some never do harness and settle down to a home life, Mol. You get one who can't commit, he'll break your heart."

She shook her head swiftly, edgily. "I don't believe that. He's had huge changes in his life since Dylan. Anyone would need some time to adjust to that."

"Uh-huh. But your heart's in the wringer as well as his, honey."

Molly would have shot back a response, but Ralph walked in, then the others. They started the staff meeting, after which she buried herself with work in her office. But just before noon, Bailey showed up at her office door.

"Flynn's still not in. You're sure you don't know where he is?"

"No, I just figured he was here by now. You called the house again?"

"No answer there. Not even the baby-sitter."

"It's not Mrs. Hanson's day to work. You tried his cell phone?"

"No answer on that, either." Bailey fidgeted with his collar. "It's not like I *have* to find him. I'm just in the middle of a project and want his two cents on an idea. And I thought—well, if there was something wrong, that he'd have called you if anyone."

So had Molly. When Bailey left, she wrapped her arms around her chest, feeling an uneasy chill skate up her spine. She'd settled that with Flynn, she knew she had. He'd let her know if there was something wrong, not keep a problem secret from her again. It was exactly what gave her hope that Flynn really loved her, that he just needed time to realize all they were together—and all they could be.

Worrying was silly, she told herself. A hundred times Flynn got concentrating on a project and forgot the time. Only Dylan was with him today—making that kind of work really unlikely—and Flynn still hadn't shown up at the office by one. Or two.

By three, Molly gave up trying to work and grabbed her coat. She'd tried calling his house a half-dozen times, and visions of accidents were bombarding her mind. She'd just reached the door when her office phone jangled. She grabbed it before the second ring.

"I'm really sorry, Mol, I realize you must have been worried—"

"Yeah, I was. Where are you? Is something wrong?"

"Not anymore. Everything's fine, but I've been at the hospital since last night. Dyl got a fever out of nowhere, shot up real high, kept climbing. It's just an ear infection, but the doc wasn't sure of that until they ran some blood work…and then they kept him until we got the fever down some. I've got him home now."

Molly sank into her chair. "You were at the hospital since last night…and you didn't call?"

"I didn't want to call and worry you in the middle of the night. And then…well, the squirt was one unhappy camper, but we were doing okay. Getting him out of there just took longer than I expected—"

"I'll come over," she said swiftly.

"No, it's okay, I don't need you." His voice was curt, strung tight with tiredness. "I can handle it, Mol. Everything's fine."

But when she hung up, she sat there frozen, thinking nothing was fine. A lump welled in her throat. Her eyes suddenly felt dry and achingly hot. She understood how beat he was, could hear the exhaustion in his voice…but still, nothing could have leveled her more than that "I don't need you."

In a scared corner of her heart, maybe she'd been waiting to hear that all along. He'd needed her when Dylan was suddenly thrown into his life, but Molly always knew he was a stronger, better man than he believed of himself. Once he realized he didn't need her anymore, why should he necessarily want to hook up with a button-down CPA for the long-term?

There was no timetable on her loving him. Pushing anyone who was going through so many changes would never have been right. And McGannon was bat-blind. About himself and his feelings.

But she'd wanted to believe that he'd see what she did.

The kind of love they had was special, rare, rich. She'd never wanted to clip his wings and tie him down, but to free him, as she felt free with him, to grow together, reaching for all they could be, respecting each other's different choices and needs.

She'd believed with her whole heart that they had a love worth fighting for.

And what hurt most of all was that she still did.

Flynn had just climbed out of the shower when he heard the doorbell. He yanked a towel from the rack, and heard the buzzer peal again—insistently, as if someone were laying a palm flat on it. He hadn't been near a clock, but it had to be past eight? Still dripping water, he peeled down the stairs, still trying to knot the towel at his waist when he reached the door.

He opened it just as a small, delicate fist was aiming for the doorbell again. The fist changed directions and poked his chest instead.

"Dammit, McGannon. If you want me out of your life, you're going to say it right to my face."

"What?" His brain registered that the whirlwind who charged past him was Molly, and it didn't take a PhD to figure out she was breathing fire and smoke. But nothing else made any sense.

"I'm going up to check on our baby—and then you and I are going to talk, buster."

As fast as she pelted up the stairs, she'd slowed down to a tiptoe by the time she entered Dylan's room. Flynn detoured to yank on a pair of jeans, and caught up with her as she was leaning over the baby's crib. Dylan was curled up with his favorite stuffed velvet football. She felt his forehead for fever, stroked back his tufty red hair.

"Warm, not hot," she whispered. "He really is okay?"

"Yeah. The fever's down to ninety-nine. And the doc said ear infections are common in tykes that size."

Her touch had been so tender and gentle, her voice so loving, that he just wasn't expecting her to turn around again with those hot-hurt, angry eyes. A thumb motioned him out. Mad or not, they both tiptoed until they were down the stairs and out of the baby's earshot.

"Mol, you're obviously really upset—"

"You bet I am! You went to the hospital without me. Without even calling me. You think I don't love that baby?"

"I know you love him. But when he woke up with that fever, it was the middle of the night. I thought I should move fast, get him right to the emergency room—"

"I can understand that. But you had time to call me, Flynn. You didn't." All that smoke and fury tensed every muscle in her body, but her shoulders were starting to droop, the hurt in her eyes far stronger than the anger. "It seemed pretty obvious you were trying to tell me that you really don't want me in your life. That you don't need me, that I'm not important to you—"

"Molly, are you out of your mind? I want to marry you, for God's sake. I want to spend the rest of my life with you. *I love you.*"

The word "marry" seemed to stop her dead in her tracks. But then she tucked her arms around her chest tightly, defensively, and started pacing around his forest green couch. "Darn it. You're scaring me. Because you sounded like you really meant that."

"I do," he said quietly, clearly. He turned on a light, and pivoted around just in time to catch the camel hair coat she peeled off and hurled at him.

"Let me give you a small tip. It's probably not a good idea to marry someone if you plan to shut them out of your life."

"The last thing on this earth I was trying to do was shut you out. There was a serious reason I didn't call."

"What?"

Flynn snagged a hand through his wet hair, afraid to take his eyes off her for even a second. He felt as if his whole life had been a test that led to this rattling moment. He'd caused that fierce, vulnerable hurt in her face. Honesty was the only way he could try healing it. "I didn't want you to think I couldn't handle my own life. I was trying to show you strength instead of weakness. I was trying to show that I take responsibility for my problems, my mistakes—and not lean on you. I was trying to earn your respect, Mol."

She stopped all that frantic pacing and went absolutely still. "Respect? How did that word suddenly get into this discussion?

"It's not suddenly. It goes back to the day you told me you were ashamed of me. Remember?"

"Flynn—that was weeks ago, months ago now. It was just a word I used when I was really upset...to find out you had a baby you didn't know about, a woman like Virginie in your life—"

"Yeah. I know. But you were right to feel that way, Mol. I was just as ashamed of myself. Shamed by what the whole problem said about my morals, my character, what I was doing with my life. And then you kept helping me. Pitching in every time I had a problem with the baby, with work. Maybe those circumstances pulled us closer... but it wasn't that easy to show you, prove to you, that I wasn't the same irresponsible jerk who got involved with Virginie. I was trying to earn your respect, Mol. Trying to earn my own. I need you to know, to believe, that I was nothing like my dad."

"Geezle beezle. I may yet kill you."

Somehow he'd hoped that pouring out his heart might inspire her to something a little different than the threat of murder. On the other hand...that ripping, raw hurt in her eyes was disappearing. And she'd first taken care to keep a couch between them, but now she stalked right to him and stabbed a finger in his chest.

"You're too damned old to be hung up on a dysfunctional childhood. Hells bells, everybody has one of those. You're not your father. You never were."

"I know that—"

"Apparently you don't. You need some risk and challenge to be happy in life, McGannon. That doesn't make you a gambler like your father is. That doesn't make you irresponsible or a user of other people or a weakling—"

"Mol—"

She wasn't about to let him get a word in. "You *do* have a problem with being an occasionally insensitive clod. If you had a brain in your head, you'd realize I was incredibly proud of you. You made a mistake with Virginie. You weren't prepared for Dylan. But you stepped up to the plate from the day that happened. You think you're the only one who's ever made a mistake?''

''No, but—''

''You don't judge someone by their mistakes. You judge them by how they handle those mistakes. You formed an unshakable bond with your son. You struggled and worked and half killed yourself to do the right thing from the first day you laid eyes on him. And you think I'm not proud of you?''

No one, but no one, could yell at him the way she did. A kiss cut her off midbellow. There were a couple of sure signs she was willing, since her arms roped around his waist and her face lifted before his aim was halfway there. Her lips trembled under his. But only for a moment.

He closed his eyes, feeling the kiss take off like a seal of the future between them. She tasted like longing and belonging. She tasted like the promise of something he thought he'd never have. ''I thought I'd lost you, Molly,'' he whispered.

''Not a chance,'' she whispered back. ''You taught me months ago that you were worth fighting for. That what we could be together was worth fighting for. I love you, Flynn.''

''Does that mean you're willing to take that big terrifying gamble and marry me?''

''I'd gamble anything with you. Haven't you figured that out yet?'' She wrapped her arms more tightly around him and reached up on tiptoe. The kiss she offered seemed to enfold him in her warmth and spirit and huge, generous heart. He wasn't so sure he'd earned that incredible rich love of hers. But there was no doubt she owned his heart…and they had a lifetime ahead for him to show her exactly how much she meant to him.

* * * * *

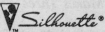

ALICIA SCOTT

Continues the twelve-book series— 36 Hours—in March 1998 with Book Nine

PARTNERS IN CRIME

The storm was over, and Detective Jack Stryker finally had a prime suspect in Grand Springs' high-profile murder case. But beautiful Josie Reynolds wasn't about to admit to the crime— nor did Jack want her to. He believed in her innocence, and he teamed up with the alluring suspect to prove it. But was he playing it by the book—or merely blinded by love?

For Jack and Josie and *all* the residents of Grand Springs, Colorado, the storm-induced blackout was just the beginning of 36 Hours that changed *everything!* You won't want to miss a single book.

Available at your favorite retail outlet.

SC36HRS9

FIVE STARS
MEAN SUCCESS

If you see the "5 Star Club" flash on a book,
it means we're introducing you to one of our
most STELLAR authors!

Every one of our Harlequin and Silhouette
authors who has sold over 5 MILLION BOOKS
has been selected for our "5 Star Club."

We've created the club so you won't miss
any of our bestsellers. So, each month
we'll be highlighting every original book within
Harlequin and Silhouette written by our
bestselling authors.

NOW THERE'S NO WAY ON EARTH OUR STARS WON'T BE SEEN!

OVER
5 MILLION
BOOKS SOLD
SPECIAL OFFER INSIDE

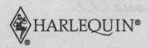 HARLEQUIN®    *Silhouette*®

COMING NEXT MONTH

Return to the Towers!

In March
New York Times bestselling author

NORA ROBERTS

brings us to the Calhouns' fabulous
Maine coast mansion and reveals the
tragic secrets hidden there for generations.

For all his degrees, Professor Max Quartermain has a
lot to learn about love—and luscious Lilah Calhoun is
just the woman to teach him. Ex-cop Holt Bradford is
as prickly as a thornbush—until Suzanna Calhoun's
special touch makes love blossom in his heart.
And all of them are caught in the race to solve
the generations-old mystery of a priceless
lost necklace…and a timeless love.

Lilah and Suzanna
THE
Calhoun Women

A special 2-in-1 edition containing
FOR THE LOVE OF LILAH and
SUZANNA'S SURRENDER

Available at your favorite retail outlet.

Silhouette®